The Blue Palm

Roy Robbins

For Linda,

Roy Robbins

randsrobbins@gmail.com

THE BLUE PALM
Copyright © 2023 Roy Robbins
All Rights Reserved.
Published by Unsolicited Press.
First Edition.

No part of this book may be used or reproduced in any manner whatsoever without written permission except in the case of brief quotations embodied in critical articles or reviews. People, places, and notions in these stories are from the author's imagination; any resemblance to real persons or events is purely coincidental.

For information contact:
Unsolicited Press
Portland, Oregon
www.unsolicitedpress.com
orders@unsolicitedpress.com
619-354-8005

Cover image: Lindsay Nolting
Cover Design: Kathryn Gerhardt
Editor: S.R. Stewart

ISBN: 978-1-956692-81-5

1.

When Delores told me after a night of glorious sex, "Don't come back," I knew I was a dead man. She meant we were through, but I thought I could not live without Delores, so I would kill myself.

My law firm's assignment to send me to Bolivia made my decision to kill myself easy. I knew there were criminal drug dealers, piranhas, anacondas, and God knows what else that could finish me off. I was sent to gather evidence in Bolivia about the growing cocaine trade, evidence for the F.B.I.'s big case.

What Delores meant was Don't ever come back to me, to the you-and-me, to us.

I had thought was forever there At the Far Cottage on the beachfront of The Blue Palm Hotel owned by her dying husband.

The only way I could do what she wanted was to die. I found out that it was, in fact, very easy to die in Bolivia.

Evaldo Hauser, my Bolivian friend from law school, had told me many stories about his home, Magdalena, a small village in the remote Beni region. But those stories did not prepare me in any way for what I would face.

If somehow, I managed to survive, I had my migraine pills and my grandfather's pistol. Twice I was in the sights of the cartel's hit man, but the time he got me in the shoulder did not kill me, a bitter disappointment to him and me.

Bolivia would make dying possible, I thought, even inevitable, and such a death would give my mother and Judge Talley (who had paid for law school), a cover story. At least she would not have a weakling son who had committed suicide because of a broken heart.

She could say that her son had drowned on his visit to the home of his law school friend, a visit that had ended tragically in a river, the Itonomas, when he was helping Evaldo's brother, Chingo, take supplies downriver to the Hauser's landing field for their private planes.

So this assignment to go to Bolivia was exactly what I needed to carry out my plan. If Bolivia did not kill me, there were other options.

I learned that the Hausers were deeply involved in the cocaine business. In fact, I learned that they wanted absolute control, and planned to eliminate their only rival, the Suárez family.

Delores had her own plan—to carry on the work of her dying husband, the wealthy philanthropist Simon Khumar, to help the Syrian orphans. She had been one herself in Syria until Khumar had rescued her. I was collateral damage in these projects, and I was very grateful that Bolivia would help me die.

My law firm had praised my work on my first assignment to collect witnesses in the case of a campus murder in north Florida. On the basis of my success, they had offered my skills to the F.B.I. In turn, they wanted me to go to Bolivia where reports about the cocaine trade were exploding.

My friendship with a Bolivian was a bonus. The fact that I had a good friend who had invited me to come and stay in Beni with his family on their cattle ranch for as long as I wanted made the assignment seem natural and would not arouse any suspicion.

By then, I had my own deadly agenda. I had no desire, no need for a life without Delores Khumar, none at all. And drowning or being attacked by rabid bats suited me just fine. A bullet would be welcomed. I went to Bolivia to die.

****

It wasn't long before I was in a large bateau on the Itonomas River with Evaldo's brother Chingo, and Chavela, one of his wives, and three other men whose names I didn't remember. Chavela had just pointed out the large "boss" monkey sleeping on a tree high above the rest of the monkey tribe chattering on the branches when she reached over and slapped my hand. I had been dragging my fingers in the water thinking of Delores.

"Piranhas," she hissed.

It was the dry season, and the river was shrinking as the water receded. I was told the crocodiles and piranhas would follow the water toward the Mamore, the large boundary river between Bolivia and Brazil, where they would wait until the rains came and then return to the smaller rivers like the Itonomas. This information was not helpful.

"But," said, "They like fingers. My aunt lost three in this river."

"Doesn't the motor scare them away?" shrugged as if to say she had tried to warn me. Her nickname was "Acid Tongue," but the indifferent lift of her shoulder conveyed the same message.

In the village, I often heard the children torment her by yelling "Where's Chingo tonight?" And someone else would add, "Chingo has more than one family."

The noise of the outboard motor made conversation almost impossible, and as I watched the wall of passing trees filled with monkeys along the bank of the river, I fell into a semi-trance to avoid what had brought me to this remote place to die.

There was something in the fierce look and words of that reminded me of Delores. When I told Delores I was leaving for Bolivia on an assignment from my law firm, she seemed relieved. Her last words constantly rang in my head, "Don't come back."

The cruelty of that command had taken me by surprise.

I can still remember standing by the open window in the Far Cottage down the beach from the Blue Palm, the sheets rumpled behind us. She was so beautiful in that early morning light and had just kissed me.

It was terrible that she was the wife of Simon Khumar, a man "as rich as Croesus," as the judge always described him. He was dying with round-the-clock nurses on duty.

It was Simon who had rescued Delores from a refugee camp in Idlib, Syria, and taken her to a Catholic school for girls who had lost their families. Simon had saved her life, and at eighteen, she married him.

He had given me a new lease on my own life when he had hired me to work at The Blue Palm every summer, saving me from my life with my mother and Judge Talley.

My first job out of law school was with Benson & Jones, a law firm with a branch office not too far from my hometown in

Clover, Florida. But after I did a competent job of interviewing witnesses, I was told to meet with my supervisor, Amaya Wheeler, who, on our first meeting, had unexpectedly asked me how well I knew Evaldo Hauser, a Bolivian who was, I would learn later, later, suspected of being connected to cocaine trafficking and the Suárez drug cartel.

The F.B.I. wanted to send someone to Bolivia to gather information on the changes in the Bolivian cocaine trafficking patterns from the Beni region of Bolivia to the States.

It was "serendipitous," as Amaya put it.

She had repeated "serendipitous" about my friendship with Evaldo Hauser, who had grown up in Beni. I had wanted to correct her and say she meant "fortuitous," but this time I I kept my mouth shut.

"Evaldo,' I explained, "was my friend in law school, and yes, we were good friends, and yes, he has invited me to visit his family in Magdalena many times."

She leaned forward to repeat the firm's intentions. "The F.B.I. wants us to loan you in a temporary capacity to go to Bolivia with your friend, Evaldo Hauser, and report on the cocaine trafficking patterns from the Beni region to the States. They know that the old routes of shipping cocaine to the States are changing and they suspect that the Hausers are deeply involved in cocaine trafficking and are looking for alternate routes.

We gave your name, Preston Ballard, to the FBI, and mentioned that your Bolivian connection might prove useful to their inquiries. The F.B.I. indicated that they would be deeply appreciative of your help. After all, you do have a connection with this remote place, and you gave Evaldo Hauser as a reference in your resume."

Two weeks later, I was on a plane headed for Bolivia. What followed, I hoped, would be my death. "Don't come back."

****

I left Cochabamba, a cosmopolitan city on the edge of the Andes plateau, around ten in the morning. We left the last of the mountains behind as we headed east toward the small village of Magdalena on the Itonomas River in the Beni. The same state that was unique in its vast stretches of pampas, much like the prairies in the Midwestern United States, except that, because of Beni's thick clay soil, much of the water did not drain off, and so much of the land in Beni was flooded for several months each year.

Evaldo also told me that several of the grass landing strips, called pistas, would have some standing water on them, but that was nothing to worry about. The trip soon turned into something like island hopping; landing and taking off at strips on the edge of small towns in the middle of the pampas.

We landed in a spray of water as we touched down in Magdalena. Evaldo was not waiting for me, as I expected. Instead, his older brother, Chingo was waiting at the small landing field as the plane taxied to a stop.

So, I was trapped with the family of my law school friend Evaldo in Magdalena, Bolivia. As far away from the world of The Blue Palm Hotel where the woman I loved had told me in so many words to drop dead.

Without Evaldo to welcome me or guide me, it looked as if I might not be able to survive. At least, I would be doing what Delores wanted.

And it helped that I had no choice but to carry out my official assignment: to gather evidence against the Suárez drug empire, and maybe their Hauser connections.

Gradually, I would piece together the Hauser's' master plan, which was to cut the Suárez brothers out of the business of processing cocaine in the Beni, so that the Hausers and other Bolivian families controlled the production, shipment, and distribution of Bolivian cocaine. The Hausers thought this would work because, I would learn later, the Suarez family was Mexican and controlled the cocaine export to the States. and so, as I gradually came to learn, were deeply resented by Bolivians, since cocaine was a native plant to Bolivia, and had been used for centuries by the local Indigenous population there. Mexico became hugely successful because of its border with the States. Evaldo had hoped to somehow to gain something from the coca produced in his native Bolivia. Why should the Mexicans profit. He wanted, I knew, to improve the cattle herds, not use them just for packing drugs..

Chingo, the brother known locally as "El Loco" put it this way: "Why should Benianos, the people of the Beni, do all the work and let the Suárez cartel get all the money?" But Evaldo emphasized that their family wanted the cocaine money not only to improve the health of the herds but to build schools and hospitals in the Beni.

Evaldo's dream was to invest in crossbreeding cattle so that herds would be able to withstand the tropical diseases that were now killing off thousands of head.

To bring all of these plans to life, the Suárezes had to be cut out of the drug business. But first, as a way of introduction to what was happening at the moment, Chingo wanted me to help with a cattle drive from Irobi, the Hauser ranch near Magdalena to San Ramón, two or three days away. But, I protested, my limit on horseback was about twenty minutes so, instead, I was to go to San Ramón with Chingo in a large dugout called a bateau loaded with supplies. It would be a river trip, according to Chingo, complete with crocodiles and anacondas, but, he joked, it was better for the "Gringo"-me- than a cattle drive on horseback.

Either way would kill me, I thought. Or at least dull the pain of Delores's last words to me until I found a better way to die.

My first day in Magdalena ended with a supper of steak, rice, and beer, followed by lessons on the correct way to string my hammock, and how to sleep in it kitty-cornered, with my head on the right side of the hammock and my feet on the left. This would level the hammock and keep me from pitching out.

As I fell asleep, I heard Evaldo's mother, Doña Angela, and the Indian servant girl, Nena, whispering in the hallway. I was just dozing off, but it sounded like Nena was saying something like "I saw the tarantula again last night. It ran into his room, and I couldn't catch it."

Doña Angela was saying something back like "Don't worry. Chingo and our guest are leaving for San Ramon in the morning.

I was just awake enough to think "I wonder if it's my room they were talking about."

But it was too late to worry now. I had been trapped by Chingo into staying up late, drinking the chichi, a sort of local corn whiskey, and I needed some sleep. I started fumbling for my watch, which I placed carefully on the floor under my hammock.

I turned on my back, thinking again of Delores's final words as I left her at the Far Cottage: "You don't understand. You can never come back. Don't come back." Time must have passed because suddenly I was wide awake. It was still dark outside. The window in my room fronted the town square and two men were outside having a violent argument. I heard the bell in the church tower strike three times. After a moment, I could hear the voices of the men arguing outside dying away.

Still on my back, I started to pull my light blanket up around me. My left arm was under the cover, and as I pulled the blanket up around me, I felt something on top of the blanket move lightly across my chest in a hesitant motion.

I froze and the movement stopped.

I gave the blanket a slight tug which was followed by another movement across my chest. I remembered Nena's saying something about a tarantula, and that "It was in the Gringo's room."

Since they had been standing outside my bedroom door, I realized that the "it" was a tarantula, and I was the Gringo.

I was at the mercy of the tarantula that night and would be at the mercy of El Loco on the river the next day. 'Good news for me.' I would not survive,' I thought, giving it my positive death wish spin.

But I had not counted on my survival instinct.

I tried waiting out the tarantula, closing my eyes and counting in slow, deliberate numbers from one to ninety-nine, waiting for the tarantula to leave or pounce. But as long as I remained motionless the tarantula was motionless.

'Was it still there?'

I gave my blanket another tug and again I could feel the slight, hesitant motion across my chest, moving toward my exposed right arm. By now, I was sweating and locked in a rictus of fear.

Desperate now, I began formulating a plan. I could grab the edge of my blanket with my left hand under the blanket and smack it down over the tarantula in one swift move, throwing the blanket against the wall. Of course, I knew that I couldn't throw the blanket more than a few feet, but perhaps if I threw it hard enough the tarantula would not have time to strike.

I closed my eyes and counted slowly, moving my hand ever so carefully beneath the blanket. Then, I grabbed a fistful of the blanket and brought it across my chest and hurled the blanket against the wall.

I rolled out of the hammock and began flailing my arms and legs in case the tarantula had not sailed clear.

After a moment, I stopped the flailing, and gradually I became aware that Doña Angela and Nena were standing in the doorway holding lighted candles and staring at me.

"Tarantula," I muttered. "Over there against the wall."

The two women glanced at each other and began slowly walking toward the wall.

After searching, Nena bent over and held up my shattered watch, which, without realizing it, I had left on top of my blanket as I fell asleep.

"I've never seen a tarantula like this," she said, in a mocking, exaggerated voice.

****

The next morning after breakfast Chingo began describing the river trip to San Ramón, where we would meet with Tico, the ranch foreman in charge of the herd of cattle that was already being driven overland to San Ramon.

I tried to tell Chingo that I had no experience on rivers. And that Evaldo had told me of the crocodiles and piranhas that lived in them, and that maybe I should stay in Magdalena and wait for Evaldo.

Chingo smiled and said not to worry because in the dry season, most of the crocs and piranhas had departed, following the receding waters as the rivers dried up.

Then, unexpectedly, Chingo's wife Chavella took my side. We had hardly spoken to each other, but I had learned how she had beaten out the local competition by getting Chingo drunk enough to marry her, and now she was saying that we should cancel the trip. "It was late in the rainy season," she said. "The river was low, and the bateau was too large. The dry season had already started, so we could not take the shortcut up the arroyo in such a large boat, since arroyo would almost certainly be dry by now, so we would have used the river landing, and walk in several hours to San Ramón. Not only that, but we would have to leave the supplies by boat and send people back with oxcarts to bring the supplies from the boat to San Ramon.

But Chingo had given her a disgusted look and said that he knew all these things, and that he had grown up in San

Ramon and that the arroyo would still have enough water float a single bateau, and besides, we really would only be carrying a small cargo of supplies. He had already taken care of everything.

Before could reply Chingo gave a quick "Let's get started' command to the gathered group and we all stood up.

With help from a few villagers, we gathered what we had to take: a few blocks of salt, several slabs of dried meat, four large ten-gallon cans of kerosene, a small five-gallon can of gasoline for our outboard motor, and two friends who wanted to go to San Ramón to see a sick relative.

I concentrated on the details for the river trip as a way to distract me from Delores and my impending death by the one lone crocodile that I was sure was waiting for me.

We all started walking toward the river with the loaded oxcart trailing behind us filled with heavy cargo. Chingo walked in front, with Chavella, whose nickname in Magdalena was 'acid tongue,' just few steps behind him, arguing in a fierce whisper that the trip was doomed and that we would end up walking in the dark from the river to the village with millions of mosquitos enjoying themselves on our exposed flesh.

Chingo said nothing until we reached the river.

We unloaded the oxcart into the large canoe-shaped river bateau and then, after the men had pushed the bateau away from the bank, we waded out and stepped into the bateau. Chingo and another man held it steady, trying to control its rocking motion, as we shifted our weight getting in.

Chingo was the last to step in, and he expertly steadied himself. Then he carefully stepped around the cargo and sat down next to the old Johnson outboard as a couple of men on the bank came forward and pushed the bateau farther out into the river.

Chingo yanked on the starter and after two or three tries, it sputtered to life and he slowly turned the bateau upriver against the current. As the men on shore cheered, Chingo lifted his hat and yelled "¡Adelante a San Ramón!"

2.

We left Magdalena at high noon, with Chingo telling us not to worry. He would get us to San Ramón well before dark.

Chavela shook her head. She knew, she muttered, that San Ramón wasn't that far away. A man on horseback could make the trip in two or three hours. But the winding river route was not as direct and our trip by bateau would take much longer.

I had thought the tarantula and my shattered watch might prepare me for what would come next, but the isolation and strangeness of Magdalena and this trip up the river, bordered by dense walls of trees and filled with strange brightly colored birds, only intensified my longing for Delores, and I became more and more aware of my lack of experience with cocaine routes, cattle, and how all this could be put together in a report for the F.B.I., and my law firm.

The Johnson outboard continued running smoothly. Chingo kept the bateau close to the riverbanks, where the current was not so strong, while the rest of us watched for signs of life along the river.

There was always something to see. The large parrots with vivid greens and yellows rose out of the trees as we approached. Chavela pointed out the torpedo wakes of freshwater dolphins called Bufeos as they hunted along the shallow margins of the river. There were monkeys in the trees high above us. Occasionally we would see the backside of a capybara, the world's largest rodent, which spent much of its life in the river.

Suddenly, Chavella turned to me with a little cry. "There he is! It's the Old Man." Everyone looked as pointed to where, high up on a limb, a large monkey was stretched out sound asleep.

"That's the head monkey. If we were to come back next week, he would still be on the same limb and still sound asleep. You can yell at him all day, but he never moves."

I looked up at the monkey again and was right. The boss monkey never moved.

Just at that moment, a man at the front end of our bateau yelled, "Hey, Chingo.

There is a lot of water up at this end."

Immediately Chingo slowed the outboard down.

"How bad is it?" Chingo yelled back.

I could see the men at the front looking down at the bottom of the bateau where the water was coming in. After a moment the man called out again.

"It's not too bad, but we need to stop and plug the leak, or we won't make it to San Ramón."

"Tell me when," Chingo yelled back.

"No problem. I know a place where we can pull in… Maybe five minutes, ten at the most."

Chingo increased our speed until the man in the front yelled "Enough! No faster."

We moved forward, with the men up front watching for a place where we could pull in. After a few minutes, one of the men yelled.

"There it is! The beach!" He pointed toward a small flat stretch of gray sand.

Chingo expertly turned the bateau, and we headed sideways across the river toward the opposite bank, moving slower and slower until just before hitting the sand.

Chingo cut the motor.

"Hold on!" he yelled.

We hit hard enough to drive the bateau into the bank, but not so hard to make the cargo break loose.

The men up front jumped out and swung the bateau parallel to the bank to minimize the push of the current.

Chingo yelled "Stand up! One at a time and step out."

went first and the rest of us followed, wading through the knee-deep water to the shore.

The damp sand that I expected turned out to be heavy, wet clay that sucked at my feet. The river has many ways to take me down, I thought.

I knew from Evaldo that most of the soil in Beni was thick, heavy clay. Which was why, in the rainy season, the water did not drain off into the rivers, but instead, formed large marshy lakes that were hidden by the grass of the pampas.

In the dry season, a man could easily travel by horseback or oxcart across the endless seas of grass, and people would point and say things like "That is the island of Huachi" where nothing was visible except the seemingly endless sea of grass. But, I would learn, that in the rainy season, while most of the land would be covered by undrained standing water, there were slightly more elevated stretches of land that would remain dry, and become 'islands,' surrounded by the 'sea' of standing water. Almost all of these 'islands' were known to the locals and had been given names. These were places where the cattle could stay dry until the rains passed, and the land dried up.

What was disconcerting to the stranger was when, in the dry season these islands 'disappeared' and became just another part of the pampas, the endless sea of grass stretching for miles in the Beni.

We landed where the receding water had left a small open stretch of level clay soil that looked like a beach, and Chingo and the crew would use the heavy clay to plug the places where the bateau was leaking. It was temporary, but it would work.

It took about three hours, first unloading the cargo to lighten the bateau and then moving it to the high riverbank where it was dry and secure.

Chingo told me to take a machete and cut small tree limbs to make a temporary platform for the cargo. Chavela took a drinking gourde and started scooping out water from the bateau, while the two men held the bateau to keep it steady. Chingo took some of the limbs I had cut and pushed them into the wet clay around the bateau, securing it against the river current and relieving the two men who were holding the bateau.

Next, we hauled the heavy blocks of salt and the fuel cans of kerosene up the steep bank. The dried meat was set on blocks of salt. Then we turned the bateau over to find the leak.

We handed the salt and the cans of kerosene hand over hand up the bank and placed them on the little square frame of limbs I had made to keep them dry, then we put the salted meat on top. Chingo removed the outboard and leaned it against a tree, along with a can of gasoline.

The bateau was heavy so there was no hope of lifting it up and holding it while making repairs, which left only one option.

There were three large poles attached to the side of the bateau for polling in shallow water. We used these to gradually pry the bateau up a few inches, and then, with all but Chavela, we propped the bateau up while one man pulled the poles out and repositioned them under the bateau.

We did the pry and lift cycle again and again until the bateau was balanced on its side and the bottom could be repaired with clay.

Chingo found a long crack in the wood and marked it with his knife on the inside of the bateau. Then we all stepped away and let the bateau drop back down, but with the bottom facing up.

The heavy clay caulked the crack in the wood from the outside with two men using a heavy tree limb to pound the clay into the crack to seal it.

The bateau was then turned over and a big mound of clay was placed over the crack inside where Chingo had marked it.

When the leak was patched, and we had rolled the bateau over the poles, back into the water, and finished reloading the cargo. But before we could step into the bateau, we heard a muffled voice upriver seeming to come out of nowhere.

"Hello there! Do you have room for one more?"

Chingo motioned for silence and yelled out "Who are you?"

"It's me. Walter."

A large tree was floating toward us, and suddenly, a man's arm appeared from out of the leaves and waved.

Everyone began laughing and yelling. It was Walter Johnson, the Protestant missionary-doctor of this part of the Beni.

His small Cessna plane had developed engine trouble and he had tried landing in a field, but his plane flipped over when the wheels caught in the tall wet grass. Not sure where he was, he had hitched a ride on the tree and started floating downriver.

As a precaution, he had put on the dark blue mechanic's suit he kept in the Cessna, folded behind his seat. Then he smeared black grease from his tool kit over his hands, face, and neck so there would be no flashes of his skin to attract the few remaining crocodiles or piranhas.

We were the first people he had seen, and he was beginning to think he would have to swim ashore and start walking.

Chingo waved to him and yelled, "Come on. You're just in time."

Don Walter evidently knew everyone and after a few slaps on our backs, he explained that with the dry season coming on he felt safe from crocs and piranhas retreating toward the larger Mamoré River.

There had been a storm in the mountains a few days before his crash, and the river was full of floating limbs and trees. Seeing a likely tree floating by he swam out and grabbed a ride, hoping to pass some men on the way who might be working near the river.

Chingo explained how our bateau had been over-loaded and had started leaking.

However, he would leave the large blocks of salt behind, covered with a tarp and with a man to stay overnight. Once we reached San Ramón, he would send the bateau back to pick up the man guarding the salt and bring him back to San Ramón.

Don Walter thought this over and then said, "I think I know where I am now. The doctor who works at the leprosarium has a house about an hour's walk down the river. I can radio for help from there."

Chingo and Don Walter thought this over and then shook hands.

"Bring Don Walter some dried meat in a bag of yucca." Chingo ordered.

A man came back with the bundle of dried meat and a gourd of water.

Don Walter clambered up the bank, turned to wave, and then disappeared.

It was clear to me that this man, trained in theology, was more skilled in the jungle than I could ever be. Not that I wanted survival skills.

Once again, we pushed off. Chingo cranked the Johnson, and we slowly turned against the current.

This would be the real test. Would the clay seal hold against the pressure of the water on the moving bateau loaded with cargo and passengers?

Chingo looked at Chavela and gave her a smile, then pointed toward the sky and Chavela began praying.

After about five minutes one of the men yelled, "Its holding!"

Everyone cheered, and so we continued up the river toward the landing at San Ramón.

I began to feel that something was wrong. I reached over and tapped Chavela's shoulder.

She turned and I whispered, "Why is everyone so quiet?"

Chavela gave me a look that said, "I tried to tell him it would be this way."

I had been amazed by the success at getting the bateau afloat and even forgot my plan for a moment to die in Bolivia. I looked at the sun, now low in the sky, and realized that we had spent over three hours fixing the leak and putting the bateau back in the water.

We were now going much slower, keeping the speed down to make sure we didn't spring another leak.

"How far is it from the landing to San Ramón?" I whispered.

"About two hours. Don't worry. Chingo will send people back in the morning for the cargo."

It was almost dark as we approached the landing.

Chingo slowed the motor, but then, as we approached the bank, Chingo, without any warning, steered the bateau to the left toward the mouth of a large arroyo that came into the river near the landing.

Everyone in the bateau started yelling at him, begging him to turn around. But Chingo yelled back for us to shut up. That he knew what he was doing.

"There's still enough water in this arroyo. I grew up here, so I know. There is a landing up this arroyo that is just a ten-minute walk to San Ramón. This will save us an hour or more of walking through the dark, and the kerosene and salt must get there tonight, not tomorrow!"

We continued up the arroyo with everyone pleading for Chingo to turn around, but he refused.

As we entered the arroyo the trees closed over us, and we were in almost complete darkness.

Chingo had a large lantern flashlight and passed it forward to the men up front to shine ahead.

And at first, it seemed that Chingo was right. We continued to slowly motor on, but soon we could tell that the arroyo was becoming too narrow and the water too shallow.

After a few narrow bends with the occasional logs bumping the sides of the bateau, we hit the bottom of the arroyo and the bateau stopped.

We sat in silence and then Chavela said, "I told him this would happen."

Chingo stood up and stepped out into the water.

"We need to lighten the bateau, so everybody out." He said.

One by one we stood up and stepped out into the water, leaving Chavela sitting in the bateau alone.

Chingo looked at her. "I said everybody."

Chavela glared back at him, then lifted her skirt and stepped out of the bateau.

Chingo laughed and said, "It could be worse."

Chavela stood looking down at the water swirling around her knees and then, in a hiss filled with venom, said, "Peor es nada." (Worse is nothing).

Chingo motioned to the men, who gave the bateau a hard shove, and now, almost a few hundred pounds lighter, the bateau floated free. We began pushing the bateau.

Chingo pointed up the arroyo and yelled, "Shine the light upfront. See that bend ahead? The bateau landing is just past it."

Almost on cue, we heard voices and a light winked back at us.

At the same time, a young boy wearing an enormous straw hat popped out of the dark and slid down the bank. With a jump, he hit the water near Chingo. Chingo picked him up and laughed as he pulled the boy's hat down over his eyes.

"And who is this little fish?" Chingo asked aloud.

The boy pushed his hat back up and smiled, "Hello, Uncle, I told them you would make it."

Chavela turned to me and said, 'Uncle' isn't the right name." Everyone laughed, knowing that the boy was probably Chingo's son by another 'wife.'

The men who had been waiting at the landing soon had the bateau unloaded and we began following the path toward San Ramón.

After about fifteen minutes, we came out of the dense jungle and walked into the small square of adobe houses that was downtown San Ramón.

In the distance, I could see flickering lights near the grass landing strip, a pista, which, Chingo had said was recently lengthened for large planes to land. There was a hut at one end for a radio operator. A frantic emu, running in circles, was chained to a stake outside.

We stopped here briefly as the cargo from our bateau was dropped off here.

Chingo and I continued on down the edge of the pista toward what looked like bonfires and a crowd of about forty or fifty people near a large shed.

Chingo started explaining what was happening. The plane carrying Arturo Suárez, and his brother Hernando, was just a few minutes way. The pilot had placed a frantic call to the radio operator in the hut we had just passed, saying that Hernando Suárez was out of his mind after multiple hits of cocaine, and would need to be restrained when their plane landed.

As we walked toward the lights and the crowd, it seemed impossible that, at least for a few hours, I had actually not thought about Delores and her declaration of loyalty to her dying husband. But even in my blank mind, her final words to me "Don't come back" had made me see deadly possibilities in the dangers of a leaking bateau on the Itonomas River. Every danger had been a gift. Maybe I could die, and soon.

I did not think about Evaldo or the law firm. These were unimportant to me in this remote land of drugs and crocodiles where I courted death, not Delores. I muttered to myself, 'I'll think about all of this later.'

I could see Chingo, who had vanished for a moment, walking toward me. I had been impressed by his competence with his crew in the river and his insistence on taking the shortcut up the arroyo.

Chingo pointed to the carcasses of recently slaughtered cattle hanging inside the large shed a few yards away from the edge of the landing field. Each carcass had been split down the spine, so the fifteen dressed steers would yield thirty sides of beef.

"Those are the cattle from Irobi, our ranch near Magdalena," Chingo went on.

"They were driven here yesterday. The men had to drive the cattle slowly so they would not lose too much weight."

I looked back at the shed, where the men with long knives were still cutting the bloody sides of beef.

"What are they doing now?" I asked, pointing toward the shed.

"They're making incisions along the rib cage. That's where we slide in the plastic bags of the cocaine paste. They grow and process the coca near the mountains."

Chingo must have seen my astonished look. He laughed and slapped me hard on the back.

"Pretty smart, don't you think?"

I tried to say something but could only manage one word.

"Damn!"

Chingo, who was enjoying this, laughed again and said, "Si, quite an operation at Irobi. I was going to take you there, but we came here instead.

"We take the coca and turn it into cocaine and package it, as you see here. Then we fly sides of beef to La Paz, remove the hidden packets, and from La Paz they're going to be shipped to a safe house near a grand hotel on the coast of Florida.

"That's where I saw the most beautiful woman I've ever seen. She was married – to the owner of the hotel. I like married women, but business is business." He laughed again. "Maybe later."

I turned away with a silent vow that nothing could prevent me from going back to Delores. And if necessary, kidnapping her, and Khumar and taking them to safety far away from The Blue Palm.

I could not leave her alone to face what I knew must be coming – the violent clash between the law and the drug dealers.

I would go back for her and convince her/force her/ kidnap her to leave with me.

I felt a flare of hope. But my dream of returning to The Blue Palm and convincing Delores to leave with me depended, in some terrible way, on my report about the events here in Bolivia. A place where people were producing the raw cocaine paste.

Now I was beginning to understand the new supply chain that would, I was sure, lead back to Florida and The Blue Palm hotel for distribution on the streets in America.

I began thinking that Australia or New Zealand would be ideal places for Delores and me and her dying husband — if only I could convince her to go.

I wanted to tell her that I admired her husband, Simon Khumar. I had started working at The Blue Palm as a teenager, and for some reason, I was told that Simon gave orders that I would have a job at the Blue Palm as long as I wanted one. And so I worked there every summer through high school and college. I didn't know that all of these dreams about Delores and things to come would be shattered.

All of this was running through my mind when Chingo described abruptly, as if he had misread my silence as insulting, mocking their efforts to create an 'all-Bolivian enterprise that would no longer depended on the Suárezes or the Mexican and Colombian cartels.

"We can't show you the whole operation now. That includes driving the cattle from one of our Irobi ranches to this landing field here.

You Gringos think we are all peasants, but Evaldo must not have told you that I am the only Hauser brother who stayed at home to be a vaquero.

"Our father studied economics at Cambridge before emigrating. Edwin studied in Chicago and was with a Wall Street firm for two years.

"Our youngest brother, Jorge, is studying engineering at Marquette. We don't know what he will do after he graduates.

"And, as you know, Evaldo studied law with you at Georgetown. He's here in Magdalena now to help our father make final decisions about how his property should be settled.

"It seems that you Americans don't know as much about how the real-world economy works, especially drugs, where money can be visible and then can go dark."

Chingo paused for a moment and then laughed.

"Like that," and pointed, as the workers continued the job of putting bags of coca paste inside the bloody carcasses.

I started connecting the fact that Chingo was throwing like darts. I began remembering the call from the D.E.A.'s office in Washington to my supervisor in Florida, ordering her to send someone to Bolivia to follow up on peculiar activities that could explain the sharp increase in the flow of cocaine to the States.

What was needed was a way to bypass Mexico and deceive the Suárezes to bring the processed cocaine to Florida via another route. This was why my friends, the Hausers in Bolivia, were useful to my office and to Washington. But who, I wondered, had connected my law school friendship with Evaldo Hauser to this recent boom in the cocaine drug trade and to me?

I knew that the Suárez brothers were Bolivians but had long and deep connections to Mexico. The Mexican cartels controlled access to the American border, and all the cocaine traffic went through them.

Maybe the Hausers were no longer willing to be their junior partners? I pondered.

Chingo's outline of what was going on in Beni became clear to me that the growing ambition of the Suárez family was to break away from the Mexican cartels and develop contacts that would go east. The Colombian port city of Cartagena had a straight shot north to the Floridian coast, making it an ideal place to transport drugs.

My guess was that the Hauser brothers wanted to do the same thing. If they broke away from the Suárez family and had their own business, they could process the cocaine from the raw coca, and be in control of the production and shipment of the finished product to America — to Florida.

For my report, I needed to understand what I was seeing and separate the truth from what might be nothing more than the unlikely and dangerous dreams of Evaldo's family.

I still don't understand why Chingo trusted me. My thought was that Evaldo had persuaded him to do so. And it was Chingo who had saved me on the river — saved all of us — but I was the one who was most helpless.

Before I could continue this train of thought any further, what looked like a two-engine passenger plane buzzed the landing field.

Chingo pointed to the plane and yelled "He's just circling the field," and ran off toward the crowd.

Almost immediately a rider galloped up and Chingo pointed toward what looked like a large pile of brush at the edge of the landing field. A man who was standing there picked up a bucket of gasoline and threw it on the brush pile, followed quickly by a rolled-up piece of burning paper.

The brush pile burst into flame. Chingo motioned to the rider, who galloped out to the center of the landing field and began firing off shots with a revolver. Other bonfires began lighting up until they formed a perfect outline marking the landing field.

Finally, three generators near the radio hut were started. Large banks of lights came on, illuminating the part of the field closest to the plane.

After everything had settled, Chingo told me he had pieced together information from the pilot about Arturo Suárez and what had happened inside the plane before it landed. Arturo Suárez and his brother Hernando were asleep in the passenger compartment.

Unbeknownst to Arturo, Hernando had taken hits of cocaine from his secret stash. When Arturo had awoken, Hernando was nonresponsive. Arturo screamed and slapped Hernando.

Startled, Hernando pulled out his gun and had aimed it at Arturo. Arturo had escaped into the cockpit.

When Arturo didn't return, Hernando waved his gun and fired off a shot, blowing a hole through the door where Arturo disappeared. The plane lurched and Hernando fell over, mumbling "I know, I know," over and over again. Arturo came storming out and tied Hernando up until the plane could land.

Restraining Hernando, Chingo told me, was one of Arturo's usual duties.

It was almost dark as Chingo and I stood waiting beside the landing field when Chingo finished telling me what he somehow knew had happened inside plane with the Suárez brothers and would be later confirmed by the pilot. The last rays of the sun were illuminating a flat plain of endless grass on the pampa near San Ramón.

Already waiting was a large cargo plane parked at the far end of the landing strip.

Several men were working there.

A rider galloped across the pampas past some grazing cattle. There was a large open shed with a tin roof. I could see women and children sitting around the cooking fires. In a corral, a few men were working some cattle. The rider came back and I heard him yell to Chingo "The plane's coming. Five minutes at the most."

Its front lights illuminating the night sky, the private plane with Hernando and Arturo Suárez banked slowly as it made its final approach toward the landing strip. The crowd around the shed surged out toward the plane as it landed. Chingo and I moved through the crowd to a slaughter pen at the back of the shed.

In the middle of the pen was a large post with a spoked wheel that turned a winch. A rope from the winch fed out of a hole at the bottom of the post and was tied around the horns of a cow at the other end of the pen. Two men were turning the wheel, winding in the rope and dragging the frantically resisting cow across the smooth, bricked floor. As the cow was pulled up to the post, the rope was tightened even more, pulling the cow's head down to the hole at the bottom of the post, until the cow was standing with its head bowed to the ground and against the post, unable to move. As soon as the cow was secured, a man by the fence stepped forward and pointed a long butchering knife at the cow's back, where the spine joined the head.

Chingo stepped out of the shadows and yelled at the man with the knife. "Wait.

We don't have time to do another one."

The man with the knife nodded and stepped back, while the two men at the wheel began to pay out the rope, freeing the cow to back away. By then, I was numb to what I was seeing. A welcome relief from my memories of Delores.

A boy about twelve came out of the darkness and stood in front of Chingo.

"Please, a head... just one."

"Who are you? Do I know you?"

"You promised me a head to take home to my mother, Carmela."

"Yes. I know you. Well... just one head then, for your sweet Mamacita. Kiss her for me."

"A thousand thanks, Don Chingo."

The boy dashed over to the row of heads, their tongues hanging out at odd angles, and their glittering eyes staring into the night. The boy snatched one up and disappeared into the darkness.

Chingo turned and walked back toward the crowd gathering at the edge of the landing strip. Inside the shed, illuminated by large kerosene lanterns, there were rows of dressed cattle carcasses hanging from ropes fixed to heavy wooden beams. Two men were finishing the bloody work.

An excited crowd had gathered at the edge of the field, waiting for the large cargo plane to taxi up. Flutes and drums played, and the crowd began singing, "Olivia Prima Rosa…"

There was a blinding glare from the plane's headlights and with a roar the plane swung sideways to the crowd and the engines were killed. Drums beat madly. There were cheers and shouts, and the horseman galloped by again, yelling and firing shots into the sky. Mothers chased their children, babies cried, and dogs were barking.

The door of the plane swung open. High on cocaine, and now freed from the ropes, the crazed Hernando Suárez apt out and started toward the cheering crowd. He raised his arms high as if the crowd were glad he was there, Arturo followed looking sour and cautious.

Chingo strode forward and the three men stared at each other, then Hernando broke away and strung out on cocaine and alcohol walked into the crowd that surged around him. A chant began to swell as ernando! Hernando fell face down, out cold."

A man fired a shotgun into the air.

I could hear Arturo Suarez yell, "Is the doctor here?"

And the answer, "He's on his way."

"Good. When we go back to the plane, have the needle ready for my brother.

Hernando's out of his head."

Hernando tried to stand on a rough bench in front of the crowd, arms raised for silence. Voices cried out, "Quiet! Let Chingo speak!"

Chingo yelled "Who lives here?!"

The crowd answered, "We do!"

Chingo bellowed, "What is your country?"

They yelled back, "Bolivia!"

"What part of Bolivia?"

"The Beni!"

"And what do you want?"

"Freedom!"

"Good! Freedom is good. And tonight, we take another step toward freedom!"

Chingo pointed to the shed where the dripping sides of beef were hanging.

"Look behind you. Tell me, where do these go from here?"

The people in the crowd looked at each other. A few men yelled out, "Not Mexico?"

As Arturo was lifting Hernando into the plane, Chingo waved his arms and yelled, "That's where it used to go. And why? Because the Mexicans want all of the Gringos' dollars. But you, my Benianos, all deserve those profits for yourselves! Tonight, for the very first time — with the help of my family, the Hauser family — proud Benianos, we will ship our product straight to the United States of America! We will bypass the Mexicans!"

The crowd roared.

"The Gringos took your tin, the Gringos took your rubber and your silver and your timber!" Chingo held his arms wide as if embracing the crowd.

"Now, the Mexicans, the Suarezes want to take this! Our coca, the true Bolivian crop. You know what I say?!"

The crowd yelled "What? Tell us!"

"¡Abajo imperialismo!"

At seeing me — the only Americano for thousands of miles — a few of the young vaqueros yelled, "Abajo con los Estados Unidos!" (Down with the United States).

The crowd roared louder, and some gave me jeering looks. Unable to stop myself, I answered back in Spanish "Abajo pantalones."

Trying to save my life by turning the violence into a joke, I yelled "Down with pants!).

Miraculously, they laughed and rushed forward, screaming, "Viva! Viva! Viva Bolivia!"

They cheered wildly as Chingo brandished a shotgun and held it above his head, Chingo then yelled "And if anyone tries to stop us from taking what is ours, we will give him this! Chingo pointed the gun up toward the sky and fired it. Surprised by the heavy kick, he almost toppled over and began compulsively squeezing the trigger, again and again, firing just over the heads of the crowd.

Chingo had warned me about the Suárez brothers: Arturo, the older watchdog, guardian, and keeper of his younger, crazy Hernando. But I was stunned by seeing the crowd rise to frenzy and thrilled to be alive because of my joke about pants had saved my life.

I was in a dangerous place, but it was offering me relief from my own demons.

The cheers turned to screams as the hanging carcasses in the shed were ripped by buckshot. Chunks of meat flew through the air and the men in the shed dropped to the floor.

Chingo waved he gun. "You are out of your mind but let's not kill anyone.

People in the crowd began standing up, laughing and whooping as they looked around to see if anyone was hurt. Then the crowd grew silent as they became aware of the headlights of the large cargo plane taxing down the runway toward the shed.

Chingo yelled, "Move back! The big cargo plane is coming up now. We're ready to load. Chingo watched the men work as they finished putting the packets of cocaine through the deep slits made in the hanging carcasses. It was a scene from hell—glaring landing lights, wild cries from the crowd, blood dripping from the slaughtered cattle containing coca paste bound for the States.

I understood more now about the ultimate plan of my Bolivian hosts. I grew more and more afraid for my friends, the Hauser family, who had opened their home to me. I was there, not as a friend, but as a spy who had been sent by my law firm to gather evidence for the F.B.I. about the drug traffic from Bolivia to the streets of America. I felt disloyal to the Hausers; trapped by all of these separate and competing forces and by my own love for Delores, who was loyal to her dying husband—not to me.

"How much longer before takeoff?!" I heard Chingo yell to the pilot over the noise of the engines.

"Half-an-hour. No more."

The cargo plane's large doors opened. Some of men began carrying carcasses into the belly of the plane. Arturo yelled up to the pilot, "Take off as soon as you're loaded.

Don't wait for me."

The pilot leaned out the window and waved. Chingo turned to me and said, "Wait here."

Then motioning, he watched d the small passenger plane with Arturo and his brother and the doctor were waiting for the doctor. Arturo and Hernando continued while the propellers began turning. The engine roared for a moment and then idled down.

Chingo stood back a few feet from the plane. behind them.

The doctor, Arturo and Hernando were lifting off, Chingo came over to me, speaking in my ear. What he said I was not able to understand, not just because of the noise from the plane's engine. But whatever he said made me feel better. Then Chingo, give me a long, hard look, signaling me to follow his lead. But I had no clue what he wanted me to do.

I wanted the doctor to give me a shot of morphine, large enough to make me see what had happened. Chingo explained later that Hernando would sleep until the next day. By the time Hernando would understand, he was in a remote ranch to dry out, it was too late. The last words he heard were that he was to go away.

I was amazed to see how Chingo had helped the doctor and Arturo get Hernando. What else would I see in this violent place where I had thought danger would numb my pain.

Chingo and I watched the plane lift off before we started walking back toward San Ramón where we would spend the night.

I heard explain Chingo what I had seen. It was put so casually it chilled my blood. I was beginning to feel that my friend Evaldo Hauser, in fact, all the Hausers, were implicated more deeply than I had understood in this plan to ship drugs to the States. The invitation to visit them in Magdalena had been presented as a favor I was offering the family-- to help take the father to a specialist. But that was not all there was to the invitation. It was certainly not what it had seemed back in Florida. And it was not as simple as my firm's assignment to go to Bolivia to gather information about the growth of the drug trade. In fact, in some ways, it was like my love for Delores, which she understood in one way, but I understood in a very different way. We all had different motives and were speaking foreign languages.

Arturo Suárez interrupted these conflicting thoughts with a hard look and said abruptly, "We thought you stole five million from our business in Mexico. But Chingo's brother, Evaldo, convinced us that it was not you but someone in the Mexican cartel."

I gave Arturo an incredulous look. "Five million! In dollars? Me? Who told you that?"

"You were lucky. It turned out to be a nobody who was working for the Mexicans, who, at gunpoint, fingered a Gringo. They all thought it had to be you, the americano friend of the Hausers."

We took a few more steps, and Arturo said, "I could use a drink."

Chingo laughed and threw his arm around Arturo. "My friend, I have a bottle that is never empty." The three of us walked into the night toward San Ramón.

I was in a state of shock. I didn't remember much after hearing how close I had come to being placed on the Mexican cartel's hit list.

I had seen the sides of beef with the bags of cocaine loaded and the plane taking off for La Paz with the beef. I would learn that it would refuel, and then fly to the port city of Cartagena in Colombia where a trawler was waiting to be loaded with the packaged cocaine. Then it would head north to Florida, to a certain hotel I knew very well from working there every summer as a teen, and owned by the husband of the woman I fell in love with. The woman who had ordered me not to return. "Don't come back."

Later, I would learn that a fishing trawler large enough for long trips on the open seas would deliver the cocaine near that same Blue Palm hotel to be concealed in the sub-basement.

When we walked into San Ramón that night, people had already started drinking.

Someone filled a big cup of chi-cha cha laced with cane alcohol and handed it to me. I drained the cup and, in a few moments, I passed out.

When I woke up, I was sitting in the corner of a room, trying not to fall over as the room kept turning around in a dizzying whirl.

I was watching Chingo arguing about when to leave the next day for the trip back to Magdalena. He had two horses in San Ramón. My Spanish wasn't good enough to follow it all, but Chingo kept saying there was no horse for el Gringo.

Chingo had not sent word ahead to bring an extra horse for me from one of his ranches.

I kept asking for someone to bring me a glass of water. Chingo said nothing, but just smiled and said there was nothing to worry about.

Chingo poured shot after shot of chi-cha into our glasses, and we gave a quick toast of "Salud," and tossed them off.

I had stopped trying to keep up and sat there wondering why I didn't see this catastrophe coming. Two horses had arrived for Arturo and Chingo the day before, but evidently, it was clear that there was no extra horse for 'el Gringo'.

The drinking, the argument about me, and the missing horse continued. After a while, I dozed off.

When I woke up, I saw that Chingo had hung his holster on a peg behind him.

Then I saw that the pistol was on the table and that a man named Luis was pleading for Chingo to calm down. Like an idiot, I sat up and in my broken Spanish said something like "Come on guys, let's all be friends."

Chingo looked at me and said something like "Fuck you!" He picked up his revolver and tried to twirl it in his hand, but he was too drunk and fumbled the move.

Luis yelled "No, no, Chingo, stay calm!" but it was too late.

The gun slipped off Chingo's finger and hit the floor hard enough to send a bullet into the bottle of chi-cha. It shattered, splattering glass and alcohol throughout the room.

The pistol shot sounded like a canon and there was a stunned silence. Then Luis leaned over, picked up the pistol, and handed it to Chingo, laughing.

"Jesus, Chingo, three people in the room and you couldn't hit one of us."

I cringed. But as it turned out, this was just the right thing to say.

Chingo laughed and threw his arm around Luis. "Maybe next time."

There was a hammock strung in a hut outside. I remember the smell of the pigsty nearby and the sound of Chingo laughing.

I slept until almost noon the next day and woke up with a splitting headache. One of the local women in the house saw me and said that Chingo and Luis had left early on the two horses, and that I was to take the bateau with the outboard and head back to Magdalena. Evidently, Arturo Suárez would soon be picked up by his private plane.

I said my goodbyes. With the help of a young boy as a guide, I found the path back to the river and began walking. I didn't know whether the outboard motor work or if the bateau leaked , or if there was enough gas to get me back to Magdalena.

The motor cranked on the first pull, and I turned down the river. Three hours later I saw the hut that was generously called the 'Port' for Magdalena. I knew a man lived there who, in the rainy season, would ferry people across the river.

3.

I had left the loading of the cocaine in San Ramón still confused about everything except my own hopeless/hopeful situation with Delores. But how would I put what I had seen in San Ramón in a report without implicating the Hausers?

In San Ramón, the whole operation was laid out in front of me, and my report would now provide useful information to the F.B.I. but would show how deeply the Hausers were involved.

The process of the harvested coca refined by local farmers by stamping the coca leaves like grapes for wine, packaging and then inserting them into the bloody carcasses of cattle and loading them on Arturo Suárez's cargo plane would be enough to convict not only the Suárezes, but also my friends the Hausers.

I had made a good guess about the supply chain from Beni to the States, one that would try to bypass the established Mexican cartel route. The Suárez family, with their long-established connections to the Mexican cartel, had controlled the cocaine drug market, but Chingo had told me the Bolivians were now demanding a greater share of the profits. A drug war had started.

The Suárez family was in charge, a fact that made the Hauser's determined to develop their own independent franchise to supply cocaine to the States by securing a safe destination for the cocaine on the Florida coast–The Blue Palm Hotel.

At that point, I didn't know, but maybe I should have known, that I might have been a casualty and that a bullet could have hit me at any time. Or Delores!

I did not know if, back then, the Suárezes had seen me then as a threat to their business. I was preoccupied with Delores and almost blind to the dangers that had been in front of me.

The Suárezes did not know that I was sent to report on their production and shipment of cocaine.

Of course, I was the low man on the team investigating it. It was my presence in Bolivia as a friend of the Hausers that had marked me, I was almost sure.

On the night that the cargo plane took off from San Ramón, I was with Chingo and Arturo Suárez. Before Chingo had corrected him, Arturo had believed I was guilty of stealing money from the Suárezes. But worse, I was, in fact, writing the report for the F.B.I. that would help convict them of trafficking drugs.

Arturo had put the wrong things together about me. And the worst thing—the F.B.I. report had been kept a secret, maybe from Chingo too. What did I know?

I needed to send a secure message to the F.B.I., asking what the plan was for me to leave Bolivia.

The radio operator relayed my messages. First to La Paz and then on to Lima and finally to Miami. My flight reservations would be waiting for me at the airline ticket office in La Paz.

La Paz was in the high Altiplano of the Andes, and its airport, at over 13,000 feet, was the highest commercial airport in the world. I knew that stepping off the plane there would literally be breathtaking—all to the good. I did not want my breath.

It was all set, so I would have a weekend with the Hausers and then fly from Magdalena to Cochabamba and then to La Paz, where I would spend the night. Then the next morning, I would leave for Lima, where I would be debriefed at our embassy about the status of the investigation before flying to Miami the next day.

I dreaded going home, and I dreaded staying in Bolivia. Worse than the my fears of the Suárez's bullet was the memory of Delores's words when she had turned her back and walked away from me that night at the Far Cottage.

How could I persuade her to take a risk and allow me to become part of her life with her husband? I knew that as long as Khumar was alive, I would have to follow Delores's lead on where to live and help her care for her husband and benefactor.

In Beni, I had been gathering information about the dangerous drug trade. It was becoming clear to complete the report, I had to just stay alive. I would be going back to Delores with no plan for staying alive and no words to convince her to make a life with me ... and her husband as long as he lived.

It was Carnival in Magdalena, and the Bolivian beer was as good as any I had tasted. I timed each sip by counting occasional noises. A dog would bark, a mother would call her children, a horse in the distance would whinny, and I would take another swallow of beer.

Behind me was the window in my room, where I had mistaken my watch for a tarantula and thrown it against the wall.

It was siesta time and Magdalena was quiet. In a few moments I would hear the cries of boys carrying wooden platters of freshly made pan de arroz made with rice flour and cheese. Then, dinner an hour later, with steak, rice and beans, and more cold beer.

I needed to change my shirt. I stood up, but outside I had thought I heard a lonely voice cry out "Don't come back!" and I swore that Delores's voice was echoing against the walls.

We had all been quiet as we sat down and began our meal. It was the most normal experience I had had in Bolivia.

Padre Liborio had been invited and said grace, and then made a joke about something political that I didn't understand. No one laughed.

Embarrassed, Chavela said she had to hurry because she wanted to talk with friends about plans for Carnival.

Then, Doña Angela apologized to Padre Liborio for Chavela's remark, saying no one had to hurry and that we should all talk and enjoy our meal.

When the dessert came and we had finished our flan with a sweet lemon sauce, Padre Liborio wiped his mouth and thanked Doña Angela for the delicious meal. Doña Angela had graciously replied how honored the Hausers were to have him for a guest.

Then Padre Liborio stood up and said, "It's time to go. I don't want to miss the bats."

I saw them smiling at what was, I guessed, the old joke that I did not understand, so I said "I'll walk with you, Padre."

On the town square, people were staring at the sky.

"It's almost time," Padre Liborio said, looking up. "The hawks are circling."

We waited for five minutes as the sky darkened, and then the first few fluttering bats appeared, suddenly rising out of the rooftops of the houses around the square where they hid during the day.

Then, other houses across the town began to yield up more bats. In a moment, it seemed, a huge stream of bats was rising upward. Circling above us and forming an ever-growing black cloud that rose higher and higher, creating the illusion that the entire town was being lifted upward.

Then, as if a switch had been thrown, the stream of bats coming out of the rooftops stopped. The enormous dark cloud of bats seemed to contract for a moment as if it were one living organism before it began rising higher. It was then that the hawks struck, diving into the edges of the cloud of bats over and over again as the dark cloud, like some wounded ship in the air, sailed slowly away.

We watched them go and Padre Liborio said, "Those are the good bats."

It turned out, he was a member of an international organization that studied bats and promoted their well-being.

The local bats that I had just seen were fruit bats that migrated at night to jungle areas in Beni. These bats did a lot of good, particularly in keeping down insects.

And, yes, he went on, there were vampire bats that roosted in places like large dead trees away from small towns like San Ramón or Baures. The vampire bats lived on the blood of wild animals and cattle and even the occasional sleeping cowboy with his blanket pulled up over his feet. The vaquero felt nothing because the saliva of the bats deadened the wound.

The vampire bats often carried rabies and were hunted and killed to save the large herds of cattle. Ranchers like the Hausers were always on the alert for reports of sick or dead cattle, which meant that infected vampire bats were nearby.

Maybe one would want my blood. Like the sleeping cowboy, I would not feel it.

People were walking around the town square, talking quietly and nodding to passing friends as they waited for the town generator to start and turn on the lights hanging from the one wire around the plaza. Then a loudspeaker was turned on and the mayor announced the schedule for Carnival, beginning with old movies. Then the names of the new King and Queen for the Carnival parade were announced, together with names of the young women who were the princesses.

In the morning Carnival would start and would continue throughout the weekend.

Competitions for horseback riding and roping, would be followed by foot races for the children and horse races for the teenage boys.

There was a dramatic pause, and the mayor said "Now comes the part filled with danger and excitement.

"A prize of one hundred dollars will be awarded to anyone brave enough to enter the ring at the edge of the town plaza where a bull will be waiting inside a pen of heavy wire. In the middle of the pen will be a pole covered in grease and at the top of the pole will be a bag holding the prize money."

Of course, I knew the old expression "Climb the greasy pole," but suddenly I realized that it was happening in a very dangerous and real way.

Finally, King Momo appeared, a skeletal figure in black and riding a white horse circling the plaza, stopping to make vicious jokes and warnings about dignitaries, and wealthy citizens, including couples cheating on each other and shopkeepers who put their thumb on the scale.

No one was exempt. And then it swept over me what I had gotten myself into with this trip to Bolivia. I had signed my death warrant. Exactly what I wanted.

I saw King Momo pointing at me and stopping. It was shocking: I had not come to Bolivia only as a friend of the Hausers but had come to report on their efforts to claim the profits from the coca crop grown by Bolivians. But claimed by the Mexicans. I had come to die. That was my real purpose. His words confirmed my thoughts.

I felt nauseous. King Momo had reminded me of what I had lived through and survived. So far.

If only one of the vampire bats would bite me.

Delores, I hoped, must have somehow known the danger I was in. Her words carried a message that I had not fully understood. They warned me: "Don't come back."

I had taken her to mean it only personally, only about our love. We were finished.

But now, I felt that she may have meant something else. That I was in danger.

There was a pop from the loudspeaker. Then, at one end of the plaza a white sheet was dropped down to serve as a screen for the night's movie. First, would be a festival of "Three

Stooges" shorts, followed by a double feature of old Mexican movies.

The plots for these movies were always the same, Chingo told me. Two caballeros about town, wearing linen suits and driving flashy cars would compete for the hand of a lovely young woman: a schoolteacher who was from a small town and had come to the big city to escape life on the ranch.

The two caballeros began to make fools of themselves, playing tricks and telling lies about each other in their efforts to impress the beautiful young woman. By the middle of the movie the audience had picked a favorite suitor and shouted encouragement to the suitor they liked.

Finally, the moment came when the young woman had to choose. There were scenes from the wedding and the happy couple driving away in a white convertible.

Only at the last moment, when the bride turned to kiss the man beside her in the car, would the audience see the face of the caballero she had chosen.

But sometimes, in a surprising twist, the young woman did not choose one of the caballeros, for out of nowhere the man she had always really loved, the poor but true-blue boyfriend she had left behind in her hometown, appeared.

He would announce that his father had discovered oil on the family ranch, making them all rich, and that he could now marry her, his lifelong sweetheart, and together they could move back home.

This fairytale plot drove a dagger into my heart. Delores would not choose me, and I would die. Not only because of my broken heart but caught in a drug war in a remote village.

For the next two days I suffered through the remaining events of Carnival, until, at the end of the last day.

Chavela and I sat watching from a bench near the Hauser's front door as a parade of young girls came by, dressed in white and carrying bouquets of flowers. This, I thought, would be the final event.

I looked at Chavela and started to stand up to leave, when unexpectedly, there was a roar from the crowd as the skeletal figure on a white horse appeared again.

Drums began beating and the crowd chanted over and over again, "Momo, Momo, Momo, King Momo tells the truth."

Chavela went running inside, slamming the door. I was thinking that she was afraid of being mocked by Momo because the crowd knew Chingo had a woman in every village in the Beni.

I sat watching, feeling sympathy for Chavela as King Momo and his drumbeating followers moved forward, stopping at almost every house for the masked King Momo to reveal some family secret or betrayal.

Finally, King Momo turned toward me. The crowd swirled around me, laughing and shouting for me, warning me, "El Gringo," to be careful.

"King Momo knows the truth and will tell everything. Even about a Gringo."

King Momo stopped in front of me, then gravely bowed. I lifted my hat in acknowledgement while thinking that it had been a good idea for Chavela to have run inside to avoid being publicly humiliated.

As if to confirm my thought, a voice came soaring out of the crowd, "Chavela, where is Chavela?"

"She's looking for Chingo," another voice replied, and cruel laughter erupted.

Then another voice answered, "He went to San Pedro to see Isabella."

Then another voice answered "No, no. He went to San Joaquin. Luisa is waiting for him."

This went on and on, with more calls for Momo to say where Chingo really was—in which village with which woman.

Then King Momo raised his arm. There was absolute silence as King Momo pointed to me and began, speaking haltingly in memorized English and pausing after each line while one of his followers gave a rough translation in Spanish:

This Gringo comes from a distant land,

He listens but doesn't understand.

We sent him home with an empty sack.

His sweetheart told him, "Don't come back."

I sat stunned.

I leaned forward as the crowd cheered and pointed their fingers at me. Then they moved on to Momo's next victims, with the drums beating their relentless and sinister ta-dah, ta-dah, ta-dah over and over again.

It was overwhelming to find myself and my secrets exposed in this remote Bolivian village, more than a thousand miles from the States. I knew that most of the people following King Momo around the square, including King Momo himself, had no idea of what his English words really meant to me, but I knew, and I understood that someone had sent me a message by this monstrous figure.

Delores was warning me and not just about our love affair's end.

The meaning was clear. I would be going home, a failure because I was too late with the information about the drug production I had seen. Too late to stop the first shipment of cocaine, sent to the Blue Palm where my "sweetheart" had ordered me not to come back.

It was clear now that even here in this remote village in Bolivia someone knew and understood the devastating and exact words Delores had said to me. King Momo had repeated her words in English to make sure I understood the warning and not just about us, but about the drug shipment and all that it meant.

I watched the crowd filter away. My pain was worse than Chavela's, for Chingo always came back to her.

That night, while gently swinging in my hammock, I tried to retrace the path that I had taken that led, step by step, to the revelations of King Momo. Things from my past that I had never connected before now began to form a pattern of relationships that had meaning only for me but were somehow mysteriously guiding everything I did.

4.

I knew somehow that King Momo's dark message not to come back was really from Delores. It took me back to another summer of betrayal, the one at Satterwhites after I had finished my first year of law school when.

I couldn't refuse to go fishing with Judge Talley because he was paying for my tuition and running my life. He had found me a job as a gopher filing papers and answering the phones in a law firm—Benson & Jones.

I had worked at the Blue Palm Hotel during the summers for four or five years, thanks not only to the judge, and I was on a first name basis with the staff. But the job at the law firm seemed a step toward a career.

My mother and Judge Talley had always seemed amused by my life at the Blue Palm where I had been the trusted "on-call" part-timer for any job. From time to time my mother would inquire about my friends and ask in an offhand way about Ann Glazer, someone I had known in the law firm staff from high school.

I would reply "We don't see each other much anymore," but then I would add, "We talk on the phone all the time." And my mother would invariably say something like "Please tell her hello for me."

One day, just before my new job at the law firm started, Judge Talley came up to me and said, "Let's take a break to go fishing."

This invitation caught me by surprise. I dreaded being with the judge in a fishing boat all day because of his relationship with my mother. My agreeing to go on the trip would only reinforce my ongoing sense of obligation to him. But, like so many other times in my life, I knew I had to say yes. I took a deep breath and then said, "When do we leave?"

"Tomorrow morning."

The judge's sense of urgency made me more reluctant and suspicious. I had stepped back, gave him a questioning look, and asked, "What's going on?"

"Khumar wants to diversify and is looking for some real estate."

There was a pause and then the judge added "I think he is looking for a place he could buy for little and then turn it into something like an elite private club where men could drink and play poker or fish while talking about business. In a very exclusive way,

of course."

"And where would this be?"

The judge smiled and said, "Satterwhites."

This sent me reeling, but at the same time it was a relief. If we were going to Satterwhites, I guessed we wouldn't be on a lake all day fishing. I had been at Satterwhite once as a boy, but I knew the judge never went there just to fish. There was another reason.

As I remembered it, Satterwhite's was nothing more than a few rundown cabins scattered through the piney woods. Back then, places like that were called "fishing camps." It was secluded on a small clear water lake, and the owner, Lem Satterwhite, had bought up the land around it.

What set it apart was the restaurant. Lem had built it on a pier that was half submerged in the lake so that the diners could look out the heavy glass windows and watch the fish they had not been able to catch swim by as they ate their supper.

As a crowning touch, the menu advertised "Satterwhites Restaurant, Home of the Mammoth Fried Fish Sandwich."

It was a fish sandwich about the size of a dinner plate, and a prize was given to anyone who could eat it all in one sitting. Lem Satterwhite would add ten dollars a week to a jackpot, which built until someone claimed the prize. When I went there as a boy with Judge Talley, the jackpot was worth several hundred dollars.

As the judge explained all this, I looked at the judge and thought, "No way that this elite resort scheme works."

The judge, seeing my skeptical look, said "It could be made to work with the kind of international money Khumar will have backing him."

"I keep hearing that Khumar is tapped out."

The judge shrugged. "Not even close. That old man has enough money in hidden accounts to get the devil out of jail.

"The investors are international; private sources in the Middle East, South America, Monte Carlo. All in offshore accounts and tax shelters. He's also got Manhattan billionaires."

To change the subject, I asked "Is Sally Booker still around?"

Sally was the long time cook at Satterwhites. Her family, she would say, had been living there since the white people killed the Indians and enslaved the Black people, including her great-grandparents. Now, she added, they just arrest us, and sometimes kill us.

Her father had been a guide and knew every snapping turtle, rattlesnake, and possum near the camp.

"I hope she'll be cooking for this new crowd."

"Sally wouldn't do it for these people, not if she knew they wanted to buy it and change it into a resort. Ruin it," the judge said.

I could tell that we were remembering the same thing. "Let's see," he continued, "First Sally would send out a bowl of pecans roasted in the oven and drenched with salted butter."

"And a big pitcher of iced tea," I added, "followed by a bowl of shrimp gumbo."

"And you had a choice of pan-fried country ham or chicken, with grits, collard greens, black-eyed peas, and biscuits with red eye gravy. Sally made the best layered cake I've ever had. For some reason, Preston, you were her favorite. 'Maybe because her own son Colson was a loser. She always made you a cake to take home, remember?"

"How could I forget?"

It really was the best cake I ever had. Sally's cake was famous, a one-two-three-four cake—one cup of butter, two of sugar, three eggs, and four cups of flour. The layers were light as a feather, and between each layer, on the top, and on the sides was an icing that she had created, with ground-up raisins and pecans in a boiled glaze made with brown sugar, heavy cream, and butter.

The judge grinned. "I was the one who deserved that cake! That was payback. I got her son Colson off with six months in rehab instead of jail. Of course, rehab just gave him a new and better market for his drugs."

The next morning the judge and I threw a few things in the car and headed toward the Georgia border. A couple of hours later and we were on blacktop roads and dodging spring-fed lakes as we tried to remember how to find the little side road where you turned off for Satterwhites.

It didn't take the judge long to find it, and soon we were on a road of white sand, weaving through the live oaks. After ten or fifteen minutes I could see a few cabins scattered through the woods.

Satterwhites camp always had a rundown look about it. But now it was much worse. Lem Satterwhite, the judge said, had made no effort to keep the camp up, and that was all for the good of bringing down the price.

After driving a few minutes through the campground area, I could see the lake glimmering through the trees as the main building came into view.

"This looks pretty bad,"

The judge nodded. "That's why we can buy it so cheap."

"We?"

"I'm one of the investors."

"So, you've already settled on a price?"

"I have a letter of intent to buy in my briefcase, with a copy of the final contract."

We stopped in front of the old office sign and waited a couple of minutes. Judge Talley blew the horn a few times and we got out.

The office door opened, and Lem Satterwhite stood looking at us, shielding his eyes. He was much heavier and had a filthy white beard over his bib overalls.

"Come on in, Judge! And bring your sidekick," he said, waving us forward.

A table and a couple of chairs were in the foyer. The front desk was in the middle of the large green rug decorated with a border of flowers. The judge pointed to the table and chairs.

"Sit there. I won't be long."

They went through the door that led to the business office. I stood there, looking around.

The door that led to the dining room was closed, but I opened it and looked at a scene so bizarre that it took me a few moments to understand what I was seeing.

The long-slanted floor that led down to the dining room was half-filled with water.

Evidently one of the submerged windows had caved in and water had poured in from the lake. Tables and chairs floated around, slowly moving in random patterns as water shifted in and out of the room.

I closed the door and walked away from the flooded dining room.

Outside, a car pulled up and its door slammed shut. A woman came in the front office carrying a cardboard box. I stood up as she came over to the table and put the box down. She gave me a big smile and said, "You're Preston, aren't you?"

"Yes..." My voice trailed off. I was almost certain of who she was, but I couldn't remember her name.

"I'm Aster, Sally Booker's daughter. She sent you this." She pointed toward the box.

"One for you and one for the judge," she said, as she lifted a napkin revealing two large cakes. "The judge told us you might be coming."

"We talked about your mother's cakes on the way here. Please tell your mother I'm grateful for the cake. I know the judge is too." I walked over to the box and breathed deeply through my nose.

"Five thin layers with brown sugar, raisins and pecans for the icing?"

Aster smiled. "Mama's cakes are always the same." There was a pause and Aster gave me a questioning look. "And how is your mother? Does she still have that pretty blonde hair?"

I could feel the muscles in my face tighten and I turned away, hoping Aster hadn't noticed.

I wasn't sure how much Aster knew about the judge's womanizing, and, in fact, I wasn't sure, either. I wasn't sure what my mother knew about the judge and his women.

All I knew was that I had always hoped that she could free herself from him, but now it was too late. We were in the same trap: we needed his money.

"Her hair is turning a little gray now and she refuses to dye it." I resisted the impulse to blurt out the truth.

My mother's hair had never been blonde. It had always been a deep, natural auburn. A fact that was well known by the locals.

"I'll be sure to say you asked about her," I had said aloud.

I knew that Aster must not have realized that Judge, had evidently brought a blonde woman with him to Satterwhites when Aster had been and introduced her as my mother.

Aster gave me a slow, careful look as she put the napkin back over the cakes.

"It's been a hard year for all of us."

"What happened?"

"Colson went back to jail."

The judge, I remembered, had recently had Colson's sentence reduced to time served and took credit for it. He had told the, mostly white, parole board that they should help make a Black life matter. Colson deserved some slack.

Though, as someone on the parole board had pointed out, the judge had always given many Black lives maximum sentences. Colson was an exception only because of Sally.

"The week after he was released," Aster added, "an undercover cop caught Colson on the street again selling weed. Mama told Judge Talley that the poor boy just couldn't help himself, but this time the judge had said: 'He had done all that he could for Colson. No second and third chances.' Now he's in jail."

I could tell that Aster understood the different levels of retribution available to the judge—ones that ran along racial and property lines. And when Aster asked about my mother's blonde hair, it may have been payback, using the judge's own rules. It was a slap to my own innocent white-boy face, and behind me, a slap at my mother.

I thought Aster's story was over, but then she went on, adding another level of meaning.

"Colson thought he could always game the system.

"The next week, just after Colson went back to jail, Luis Pandero, the son of another immigrant family our church helped, was killed in a boating accident.

"Luis had spent a lot of time at our house. Mama had bought him a pair of Nikes and made her cake for his birthday."

"How did it happen?" I asked, wondering what Aster's story meant regarding me and my mother.

"Luis was trying to show off his Nikes and boat was going too fast. He stood up and lost his balance. The boat flipped him out, but the propeller blades caught his ankle and chewed his leg up. He went under right away.

"As I said, Mama was really close to him, and Lem Satterwhite had promised Luis a job as a dishwasher. I think Luis was really excited about it. They dredged the lake but never found him."

I couldn't help but wonder if Luis had a connection with the drug dealers on the streets and if Colson had hoped these connections might be a path to acquiring more drugs. But now Luis was dead, and Colson was back in jail.

Aster took a step toward the door and then turned, looking at the cakes. "Those are the first cakes Mama has made in a long time. She said that if I saw you, to tell you to watch your back. I don't know what she meant." Aster smiled.

"People say she can see what's coming." She laughed in a bitter kind of way and added, "I wish I had listened to her about that last man I was wasting time with."

Before I could say anything, we heard Lem Satterwhite and the judge yelling at each other. Aster looked at me and shook her head.

"Don't say anything about Colson or Luis. I need to hurry. Make sure you get your cakes."

Then she was gone.

I wanted to walk Aster to her car, but Judge Talley and Lem Satterwhite came storming out of the office.

Satterwhite was yelling that he had to have more money, and the land itself was worth more than eighty thousand.

"You're lucky to get that," the judge snarled. It will cost more than eighty thousand to bulldoze this pile of junk. The judge saw the cakes and leaned over and inhaled, then turned to me.

"When did Sally bring these?"

"She didn't come herself. It was Aster. Sally wasn't able to come."

"She can barely walk," Satterwhite added, calming down.

The judge turned to me.

"Are you ready?"

Satterwhite held up his hand. "Wait a minute. What about my money?"

The judge pulled out his cell phone and talked for a minute. "We'll wire you the money in a few days."

We left Satterwhite standing in the middle of the room.

"You drive," the judge ordered me when we got to the car. "I've got some calls to make."

He got in the back seat with the box of cakes. I started the engine and we drove away, passing the ramshackle cabins until we reached the blacktop road. I turned on the radio and found a country music station, making it loud enough so I couldn't hear the judge talking. The first song up was "Your Cheating Heart."

As I settled down for the long drive home I began reliving in my mind the visit to Satterwhites, trying to sort out what I had heard and seen. The flooded dining room, Colson's situation, Luis' death, Aster's double talk, the judge's land deal/scheme, Sally's warning to watch my back, and Aster's question about my mother's "pretty blonde" hair.

Like so many times before, I was angry about my mother's compromised relationship with the judge. I hated to admit it, but I had benefitted from this.

Was I a pimp for my mother, taking money for tuition and a job in return for her staying with the judge?

It seemed that my entire life was split in two: betrayal and accommodation to it for a price. Everything I did had to be viewed through the lens of how my actions might affect my mother and me.

I would have to deal with the judge as I always had, but now with what I had learned at Satterwhites. Not only about the judge's betrayal of my mother with the "blonde" but also about the plan to buy Satterwhites on the cheap and turn it into a paradise for the international set intent on hiding the wealth. I had refused to see how I benefitted from my mother's betrayal.

The high flying one-percenters the judge was counting on would not be caught dead in north Florida, no matter what the judge claimed. So what was the real plan?

Then, I wanted to know, why would the judge and his crowd keep pretending that the Blue Palm Hotel could also become a destination hotel again?

And what about the beautiful and mysterious Delores? People kept talking about her at the hotel, but at that time, I had not yet met her. I didn't know the answers, but as we drove toward home I calmed down. Soon I would be filing and answering the phone on the job at the law firm arranged for me by the judge.

On the long drive back, I asked the judge about Khumar, whom very few people had ever seen.

Khumar, the judge said, had hired him several years ago to assist him in a difficult immigration case, which involved Khumar trying to bring his wife to America.

The judge did not reveal all the details, only to say that Simon Khumar's wife was much younger and, the judge had heard, she was very beautiful.

Ann Glazer, my old friend who had recommended me for my first summer job at the Blue Palm, later confirmed this. And now this beautiful woman had broken my heart and ordered me to never see her again.

How could I do that?

5.

I learned from Ann Glazer that Delores Khumar had studied in Paris, but I did not know how she got there from the Middle East, a story I heard later.

Judge Talley had thrown himself into her immigration case and after a few months, and strings pulled, Khumar's wife was on her way from Paris to Florida.

This was the beautiful woman who would turn my world upside down and make me want to die in Bolivia, or anywhere.

I had just finished an interview that the judge arranged with a mid-level law firm who offered me a summer job as a gopher. I was told it might lead to a full-time position after I finished law school and passed the bar.

I had gone back to the Blue Palm Hotel to say I would not be working there for the summer. Before I left, Sandy Lefcourt, the manager, asked if I would stay a few more days to help move meat down to the lockers in the sub-basement.

This is how I first met Delores.

That day I was wearing a bloody butcher's apron, and I was taking a cart of meat down to the freezers in one of the storage rooms. The ancient service elevator was manually operated. I had just started down to the subbasement when there was a buzz and the light for the lobby floor lit up. I opened the door and Delores was standing there.

She was clutching a white envelope in her hands and gave me a nervous look, then looked down at the envelope.

"Are you...Preston?"

"Yes. Preston Ballard."

She glanced at me and didn't seem impressed with what she saw. "You're very young."

"So are you."

She stepped inside and handed me the envelope. "Simon said to give you this."

I waited for some explanation, but she turned away. I stood looking at her, transfixed by the sudden appearance of the most beautiful woman I had ever seen.

"Is the elevator broken?" She was looking at the door.

"No, it's on manual."

"I see."

"It's an old elevator. You have to tell me where you want to go."

"Oh." She took a deep breath and gave me an exasperated what's-wrong-with-you kind of look. "Well, where are you going?"

"I'm going to the sub-basement."

"I've never been to the sub-basement. What's down there?"

"Oh, almost everything the hotel needs to keep operating." I pointed toward the cart. "These are sides of beef that need go into a cold locker."

She looked down. "Hmm," as if considering something, then nodded toward my blood-stained apron. "So, you're our butcher?"

"No, I did a lot of odd jobs for the Blue Palm. Wherever help was needed. But now I am almost done with law school and will be working part-time in a law firm. I start in a few days."

She smiled and nodded. "That's what Simon thought would happen." She seemed delighted to have her husband's words confirmed. She held out her hand.

"I'm Delores Khumar."

My hands were smeared with blood from unloading the beef. "We can shake hands later."

"Thank you. I'd like that."

I liked it too. I liked the way she looked at my hands and didn't pretend to be shocked. I liked her lilting accent, her curiosity, and the amused way she looked at me as if she could read my mind. I tried to stop staring at her and say something clever, but nothing came.

I had guessed we were about the same age.

As I started to close the elevator doors, I heard her say in a sharp preemptory voice. "Well!"

I stopped, not sure what she meant.

"Is something wrong?"

She pointed to the white envelope I had put in my back pocket.

"Aren't you going to read it?"

"Of course," I stammered. "Is it urgent?"

"Simon sent it to you." she raised her eyebrows, as if that explained everything.

I wiped my hands and opened the envelope.

I was to meet Sandy Lefcourt, at the bar near the elevator on the first floor.

I thought that probably the bar was running low on the Johnnie Walker Black, or there was a guest with a special request.

I explained to Mrs. Khumar that I couldn't very well leave a cart filled with cuts of beef on the elevator, so we went down to the sub-basement. I unloaded the beef, then we came back up to the first floor. As I turned to go I felt a tug at my sleeve.

"Thank you again for the tour of the sub-basement. You should go wash up."

She was looking at me and I was staring at her.

"You're welcome."

"Perhaps you could help me," she added, almost as an afterthought.

I didn't have any idea what she meant, but after just one elevator ride with her, I would have gone anywhere, done anything. But I was just part-time help and did not know anything.

"Sure," I said. "I'll be glad to help, if I can,"

"Simon wants me to be more involved in his hotel business. He wants to put the Blue Palm on the National Registry of Historic Buildings and has asked me to write a proposal. You're finishing up…?"

"Law school, but I just started."

Delores nodded. "He needs me to take over the books. Investments, expenses, and other things I'm not sure about. He wants you to help me. Can you start soon?"

"I'm sure the hotel has an accounting firm for all that. You should talk to those people. And, I have a job that I will start in three weeks."

There was another flustered and impatient look.

"We do, of course, have a firm handling the books. But Simon wants me to organize all of that in-house, but in a different way. You see, my job isn't really about the money-making part of the hotel. Although, to tell you the truth, we haven't been doing a good job with that either.

"I'm really not making too much sense, am I?"

"You could start by telling me what, exactly your husband wants me to do. And as I said," I reiterated a little agitated, "I have only three weeks free to help you before I start working for the law firm."

"Simon loves history…" she hesitated, searching for the right word.

Before she could finish, I said, "And beautiful things."

She looked startled and gave me a questioning look.

"Yes, he does. How did you know that?"

"It's obvious, from the rugs and paintings in the hotel." I was looking back at her sheepishly, "not that I am saying that you are like one of those."

There was a wonderful moment as my double meaning had not registered at first.

I could tell she wasn't upset because she laughed and said she had been called worse.

"So, are you interested in the job or not, even for two weeks? I need to know."

I had already decided to take the job, if for no other reason than the chance to see her every day, even for just two weeks. Still, I had to be careful. I waited.

"Would two weeks help? After that, I'll be working in Daytona. But I can work two weeks here."

"Tomorrow, at nine."

I hesitated, "I'm not sure if I'm the right person for what your husband needs."

"Well, Simon and Judge Talley think you are." Delores gave me a glimmer of a smile and took a step closer.

"And now…" She flicked her hand as if waving away a thought. "Now that we've met, I'm sure you are the person for this project."

The effect, as Delores moved closer, was magic. So powerful that I hardly took in that Judge Talley had been in on this two-week job at the hotel, as well as the law firm.

It was as if my entire body and soul had been magnetized and that, unable to stop, I was being drawn toward her. I took a breath and stepped back. I was sure that Delores understood what was happening and that this wasn't the first time that a man had been drawn to her that way.

Delores seemed to know what I was feeling, and, turning her head away, she stepped back.

"Simon suggested that you and I should meet about his concerns and draw up a plan on how we should proceed. Would that work for you?"

All I could manage was a weak "If that is what he wants, I guess I can give it a try."

Splendid!" Delores was changing in front of me from Helen of Troy to a brisk office manager.

"We can have our first meeting tomorrow at nine. You know the hotel better than I do. Pick out one or two areas where we need immediate improvements."

Delores put out her hand. All I could do was look at it. She slowly reached out her other hand and placed my blood smeared hand in hers. "We'll shake hands to, how does it go, seal the deal?"

I turned to leave and was stopped by another one of her preemptory orders.

"Oh, and by the way, we're blooded friends now, and my friends call me Delores."

I left in a daze, feeling like a schoolboy who suddenly realizes that what he has agreed to might have serious consequences. How did it all fit together?

My meeting with Delores in the elevator started off simply enough, I thought. She was a beautiful woman, and I would work with her for two weeks.

Why not?

Then I remembered the note from Khumar with the request for me to meet Sandy Lefcourt.

My thoughts were racing now, and I realized Delores had let slip that Judge Talley was involved in this job offer at the hotel, the same man who took me to Satterwhites and had taken a blonde there and introduced her as his wife.

All was not what it seemed. Judge Talley was not my benefactor. There was a hidden motive, maybe just to keep me from talking to my mother about "the blonde" at Satterwhites...

I thought of Delores, and the way she didn't walk but floated with no effort, and how the magic of her gaze stopped me from thinking.

****

The Far Cottage became our office for two weeks. We began working not on the books but on plans to restore the Blue Palm to its 1920's glory, back in the early days of the first Florida boom. But soon — the second day — in the most natural and passionate way, we became lovers.

During the day we put together all the documents required by the National Registry of Historic Buildings, I heard the story of how she and Simon had met and that they now lived on the top floor of the hotel in a large apartment. Everything they needed was made immediately available at the touch of a button. She began by telling me how she pressed her thumb on the security pad, waited for the door to click open to let her in their darkened rooms. Simon had an aversion to bright lights and so they lived in a perpetual twilight isolated from the world below.

The Far Cottage gave us a refuge where we were free to make love and tell each other our histories. I came to hope we would have a life together. When I went to the Far Cottage to be with Delores, I felt I heard the first joyous lines of an old song celebrating Bonnie Prince Charley's escape to the Isle of Skye:

Speed, bonnie boat, like a bird on the wing

Onward! the sailors cry,

Carry the lad that's born to be King

Over the sea to Skye.

I learned this song from my Glee Club teacher in the seventh grade. She was from Scotland and had come to America to take courses on international finances. She was always singing it and told us she longed to return to Scotland where she had left a bonnie lad behind.

Going to meet Delores in the Far Cottage for those two weeks before I left to work in Daytona was both heaven and hell. I knew I had to leave Delores and take the job the judge had arranged for me, and I didn't understand the hell it opened until our last night together.

In those hours with Delores in the Far Cottage, I did not know that later in law school I would become friends with Evaldo Hauser from Bolivia, where a target would be put on my back.

These are only wild fantasies of what might have been—a life with Delores.

6.

Betrayal and treachery were the last things on my mind as Delores and I had begun our love affair.

Aster's casual remark about my mother's 'blonde hair' had been still preying on me, revealing the judge's serial infidelities and my mother's degradation. A degradation that over the years paid for my college and law school.

At the Far Cottage I experienced love and passion with Delores, like drugs similar to the kind Circe had given Odysseus to keep him from going back to his responsibilities of running Ithaca.

I thought the Far Cottage would be our Isle of Skye, but the reality was different,

It was a new life sealed off from reality.

Delores said she had never questioned Simon. He had immediately understood her fears.

The violence in Syria had torn apart her sense of a world of order and safety, made her an orphan. Here at The Blue Palm her husband had created a world that could be maintained within a structure of security and civility. Except, of course, it was an artificial world, and she would always sense that the real world was lurking. Even in the softly lit endless corridors at the Blue Palm, which Simon had taught her to navigate as she carried out duties she assigned herself as tokens of gratitude to the man who had saved her.

What she revealed about her past life in a Syrian refugee camp after her parents were killed, and then in a Catholic orphanage in Paris, made me almost afraid to touch her. It was in the refugee camp that she learned to hoard food and to betray others to avoid punishment.

Sudden noises, cars backfiring, even a dropped glass would always make freeze her where she stood, halted by a wave of fear.

Later, in the Catholic school, she would report anyone to the nuns who broke a rule, especially the rules about stealing food. She warned me as she kissed me that she was dangerous. Not evil, but certainly dangerous.

She had been brought to Paris via a rescue mission that Simon funded and had often visited. She was sent to a Catholic school for girls, and one day, when he came to admire the new kitchen, he heard a muffled noise and found Delores kneeling in a closet, stuffing bread in her pocket.

She was humiliated and tried to blame a younger girl for the theft of the bread.

Simon immediately understood because he had grown up in post war Germany where stealing bread could get a person killed.

"My name is Simon," he said, as he slowly approached her. "Can I come and visit you again?"

He had turned to the nuns. "That is, if these two good Sisters would permit it."

Delores, who had been expecting the worst, watched Simon in amazement.

"Tell me," he asked, turning back to Delores, "Why were you hiding in the closet?"

Now Delores understood what was happening, and automatically said, "Felicia made me do it. She stuffed the roll in my pocket and pushed me into the closet."

"Not true, Delores, not true," one of the nuns murmured.

But Simon leaned closer to Delores. "Don't worry, I've had to say things just like that. Sometimes, you have to do what you have to do. Isn't that right?"

Stunned that she finally had met someone who understood, Delores whispered back, "I don't want Felicia to get punished."

The two Sisters nodded. "We will speak to the Mother Superior about it."

Simon's visits had continued until her graduation. Delores was a gifted linguist, and, with Simon's help, she worked as a translator in a large publishing firm. She was able to do the work, but only if she knew that Simon was nearby. They were married two years later, and Simon, now living at the Blue Palm, had used Judge Talley to secure her immigration papers.

Delores told me that her only assets were the classic ones: She had a deep intelligence that she knew how to hide. Her beauty, she had learned to pretend, didn't exist. If pushed into a corner, her confidence would vanish, and she would turn into the cringing waif from the Syrian camps who was willing to betray anyone if deemed necessary.

In the Far Cottage, I learned her harrowing story and of her utter devotion to Simon, as well as to their marriage. He had saved her, not only from terrorists, but from herself.

But I knew that I had rescued her in other ways. With tears in her eyes she told me that Simon had been given six months to live, even with treatments from Johns Hopkins for pancreatic cancer.

Delores began talking about the camps where she had lived. "All the camps," she said, "were pretty much the same: Hell."

We had spent the afternoon working at the Far Cottage and now were in bed listening to the waves. I turned to Delores and looked at her, counting the reasons I loved her.

She looked up. "You can't really understand, can you?"

"A part of it, maybe. I've read about the camps in Syria, but I can't imagine you in the camps.

"I don't remember my father at all. I lived with my mother in a camp. She was killed by an air raid just before Simon found me. After that, I lived most of the time in the schools Simon chose for me.

"The nuns were in charge. I learned English, French, and accounting, but I never thought of those places as schools. There was no freedom. It was more like a military operation. We actually marched to class."

"You've been homeless in Syria and a student in Catholic boarding schools, and now you are at the Blue Palm." I summarized.

"The people in the hotels are all strangers to each other.

"In Europe I was not quite a refugee because of Simon, who had money and powerful friends. I don't remember their names because they changed so often. I keep thinking I might meet some of them here, at the Blue Palm, but so far I never have."

"What helps you here?"

Delores paused.

"There is a melancholy atmosphere about it, a silence in this old hotel late at night. Sometimes it seems to grow and become a living thing. I can hear the muffled sounds of people talking in other rooms, and this becomes mixed with the idiocy of distant noises, like the water draining out of a bathtub, or a toilet flushing. The furniture seems ancient and strange. The light from the lamps isn't friendly but is muted: a dirty yellow without warmth.

"Simon likes it because, except for a few of the older crowd, it keeps people away. It loses money every year, but he can afford it.

"How does that make you feel? Are you still afraid?"

"No, but there is something sad about it, but most of the time I am not afraid.

Simon feels it too and tries to put it out of his mind with a project like this restoration.

"Think of it as a tax haven. What makes it work is that it's on island, accessible only to those who know about it and are comfortable here. It's an old hotel that I am sure has great potential."

Delores paused, and then added, "I think Sandy Lefcourt feels the same way:

Improve the Blue Palm but don't change it. He calls it 'The Old Gray Lady'. Simon wants it recognized, but still not just as a place for those who like spas and yoga classes. He wants it on the National Register. That's how you will help me."

We were quiet for a moment and listened to each other breathe.

"What about Simon?"

"Simon understands, up to a point."

"Is that all?"

"Oh no!" She smiled as if remembering something. "Simon has his routines to help him and I. Everything must be done by the rules. From eating dinner, to dressing, to setting goals for myself. Rules that apply to him as well.

"He does that because he wants me to know that here, life can have a structure. That there are rules to follow, and if you follow them you can be safe from hidden attacks. I am trying to learn how to trust myself."

Delores paused, as if remembering something. "But no one is ever safe. Have you ever read 'The Magic Mountain'?"

"No. What's it about?"

"It's about a man who lives in a sanatorium for T.B. patients. I'm trying to arrange to have Simon admitted to one in the French Alps, to have his pancreatic cancer treated. I haven't told him yet."

I sat there, not knowing what to say.

"How long?"

"The doctors aren't sure. There are treatments for it if you catch it early, but Simon kept it hidden for a long time, so we don't know."

"Will you stay here?"

"There is nothing here that I can identify with."

"Can you identify with me?"

Delores sat up and gave me a hard look.

"How is that possible? In Syria, there were no rules. When I heard a bomb falling it wasn't personal. No one was saying 'This bomb is for Delores.' It was just a bomb coming down. Maybe it would kill me, maybe not.

"Here, you live by rules that you can understand. You may not like them, and they may be wrong, but you know what they are. You can decide how to deal with them.

"Simon survived the Holocaust and understands violence. He knows how to respond to it. Not with more violence but with funding to build places that are safer than tents at my home in Ras al-Ayn on the Syrian-Turkish border.

"He says the blood of many empires flows in his veins and he feels responsible to help the victims, whoever and wherever they are.

"People are starving and turning against each other, in part, because of U.S. sanctions. It is a war, not like the war in Iraq where there were soldiers in uniform who hunted down Saddam, but a war of starvation, attrition, hidden behind the name 'Civilian Protection Act.'

"A war by other means. And which, unlike bombs, kills even more effectively because it targets the entire population. The children are the first to die. I was lucky."

Delores looked at me, alert and suspicious. "Why aren't you telling me more about you? I have told you a lot about me."

I took a deep breath.

"It's hard to put into words. I don't have a sense of my own identity. Maybe it's because my father died just after I was born, and I've never been close to my own mother. She lives by invisible rules. She says there are always rules. But the important rules are the ones no one talks about; the rules that are unconscious and hidden."

"How did you survive?"

"I never questioned or confronted her."

"Can you give me an example of those rules?"

"Yes, I can." I paused, then said, "I love you. That's all I can think of when I'm with you."

Delores threw the covers off the bed and stood up and turned away. She began putting on her clothes.

"Tell this story of invisible rules."

"My mother says that the important rules are the ones no one talks about; the rules that are unconscious and hidden in your mind. The rules beneath the rules."

By the time I finished dressing, Delores had poured herself a drink and was standing by the window. I saw her watching the ocean, where a dark rain cloud was moving slowly across the horizon.

I came over and stood beside her. She moved away, not looking at me. There was nothing else left to do but to tell her.

"I got a call last night. My firm is involved in a drug case. They want me to go to

Bolivia."

Delores gave a small cry. "No! I don't want to hear that!"

"They just need me to confirm some information. It will only take a few weeks."

"You're crazy. They'll be waiting to kill you when and if you come back."

"People are depending on me. I had a friend in law school who was from the part of Bolivia where I need to go. He's in Washington now, on family business. His father has cancer. He called and asked me to help him take his father to meet with a doctor, one in Brazil. And then, he invited me to come for a longer visit to his home in the village of Magdalena even though he could not get there for a while.

"People at work were talking about Bolivia, and I just mentioned that I knew someone who lived there. It's just a horrible coincidence."

"You're going to Bolivia to report on something you do not know about. You could be killed. Is this one of your hidden rules?"

"I trust my friend, Evaldo Hauser. I've known him for some time."

Delores turned away. "If you go, then don't come back."

She was trembling. I pulled her to me and said, "Let me tell a story about my mother. I've never been sure what it means."

"What story is that?

"It happened when I was ten years old. It's about Blue Jays." We sat at the table, sipping our drinks and looking at the ocean, with the sequent waves punctuating my words as I started to tell the story.

I was still stunned by Delores saying, "If you go, then don't come back."

To avoid or delay what Delores meant, I launched into a story that would not explain my life but might show what it was like to be the son of a woman who lived by unspoken and mysterious rules that controlled the universe. Her universe and mine.

I hoped I could make Delores understand.

I grew up learning how to hide the truth, or, more accurately, learning how to tell the truth by telling half-truths. For example, if someone asked about my mother's relationship with Judge Talley, I learned to assume a bored, dismissive voice and say,

"Yes, Judge Talley is a good friend."

And this was true, but it wasn't all of the truth. While the judge was extending his right hand of friendship toward me, he directed my attention away from his left hand; the one of control and manipulation that he kept out of sight.

As a boy, I needed lessons that would help me follow these rules, but my mother and Judge Talley never explained them.

"We always made a yearly visit to Georgia where the judge had grown up, and where most of the extensive Talley clan still live. The judge's older brother, Uncle Virgil, lived there with Aunt.

"They lived in a twenty-three-room clapboard home that began as a plantation house and was then turned into a country store when an addition was built in front of the home. There were enormous rooms, with winding hallways that led me in circles back to a cavernous ballroom, which was empty except for a grand piano, pushed up against the wall, and scarred.

"Uncle Virgil told me that his old family home was spared because the Yankees needed it for their headquarters.

"Uncle Virgil was obsessively frugal, saving balls of string, rolling cigarettes of rabbit tobacco, and shifting down to neutral to coast downhill to save half of cup of gas and every penny.

"As the younger brother, Judge Talley had learned that the up-and-coming state of Florida offered greener pastures and room to expand. Satterwhites in north Florida is his current big project and I think Simon may have backed it.

"Virgil's wife, Aunt, was as frugal as her husband. After the noon meal of pinto beans and cornbread, my mother learned that feigning headaches was her way to escape for the afternoon and avoid any questions about marrying the judge.

Fortunately, Judge Talley backed her up about the headaches, and after a morning of shelling butterbeans and peeling peaches, my mother would flee to her room clutching her head as she felt a migraine coming on. Then the judge would say, 'She's been to the doctors, but they just give her medication for the pain.'

"Uncle Virgil and Aunt had no children, so I was left at loose ends. Luckily, a neighboring family, the Jacksons, had a son called Junior.

"I understood that Junior was, as Uncle Virgil explained, 'slow', or as Junior's mother put it 'thoughtful.' At the time, Junior was about twelve and I was eight, and we soon became fast friends, wandering for hours through the Georgia pines looking for something to shoot at with our B.B. guns.

"Uncle Virgil had a large grove of pecan trees away from the house, but there was one near enough to provide shade for the back yard. As his pecans ripened they were attacked by Blue Jays that waited until the soft green outer husks had formed, but not yet hardened. Then the Blue Jays would puncture the outer early husks with their sharp beaks and then leave the ruined pecans behind.

"The grove away from the house had enough trees to survive the Blue Jay's attacks, but the pecans in the big tree near the back yard would be ruined. Uncle Virgil saw the Blue Jays as his personal enemies.

"He would leave his old single shot .22 rifle just inside the slightly open back door, where he would stand for hours. When the Jays appeared he would gradually slide his rifle through the slightly opened back door and squeeze off a shot.

"The pecan tree was about twenty yards behind the house, so it was a tough shot to make, and even when Uncle Virgil managed to hit one of the Jays, they would soon come gliding back to the pecan tree.

"This routine could continue all day through the summer, with Uncle Virgil becoming more and more frustrated. Judge Talley would often stand behind Uncle Virgil and pretend to encourage him, slapping him on the shoulder at the almost inevitable missed shot and murmuring 'You'll get one next time.'

"Uncle Virgil's routine of stalking Blue Jays continued for most of our visit and after a couple of days of random gunfire my mother became unnerved. The house would be quiet for long stretches during the day and my mother would forget that Uncle Virgil was standing at the door with his rifle.

"Inevitably, it would seem, just when mother would stand up to help clear away the dishes left on the table after lunch, there would be a loud crack as Uncle Virgil fired off a shot, followed by a cry from my mother and a shriek of rage from Uncle Virgil as the Blue Jays disappeared into the nearby trees.

"One day, while Junior and I were moving through the woods with our B.B. guns at the ready, I tried to explain Uncle

Virgil's rage at Blue Jays. Junior listened, nodding his head and said, "I hate Blue Jays too." Then holding up his B.B. gun, 'Let's kill a few for him.'

"Junior, it turned out was a bad shot and after a few days we still had an empty bag with no dead Blue Jays inside. Finally, after a long patrol through the woods, Junior saw a row of fledgling Blue Jays, not quite old enough to leave the nest and fly away.

They were standing exposed on a limb, trying to decide to take that first jump off.

"Without hesitating, we popped away with our B.B. guns at close range, until there were four dead blue jays in our burlap bag. Triumphant, we headed back to Uncle Virgil's house, knowing how pleased Uncle Virgil would be when we showed up with our bag of dead birds.

Aunt had not come back from her weekly trip to the grocery store when Junior and I came in. Junior and I emptied out the bag of dead Blue Jays on the kitchen table and I said, "I'll bet this will make Uncle Virgil happy now."

My mother looked at the dead birds, "Yes, I expect it will." Then looking at Junior she said, "You go on home now."

"Yes ma'am," Junior reached the back door and turned, "Maybe we can find some more Blue Jays tomorrow."

My mother said nothing as Junior went out the back door, and then she turned to me and said, "Go upstairs and wash and change your clothes while I finish cooking. And don't say anything about these birds."

"Why..." I started to say, but she shook her head and said, "It will be a surprise.

Just take your time. Remember, you have to finish your book before we leave for home.

What's the name of the book you're reading?"

"The Swiss Family Robinson," I said, knowing this was just a little test.

"And how many more chapters to go?"

"Three," I said.

I could hear Aunt's car door slam and hear Judge Talley and Uncle Virgil coming in from the garage. The next thing I knew Judge Talley was calling that dinner was ready. It was almost dark as I sat down. I reached for a large bowl of butterbeans, but my mother came up behind me and pushed her finger hard into my back.

"You have to wait."

I could tell from her voice that something was wrong. I realized that the others were in on to whatever it was that was about to happen. I watched her as she went over to the oven, pulled out a covered baking dish and set it down in front of me. Then she lifted the cover and said, "This is for you."

I could see four headless, perfectly dressed small birds, with their feet tied together by a string and roasted.

My mother pointed at the birds.

"This is what you brought home this afternoon. Eat them."

I took a few bites but started to gag, and I began running toward the back door, but I couldn't make it, and I vomited on the floor.

Judge Talley appeared and grabbed me by the back of my shirt and sent me flying out into the back yard. Uncle Virgil began yelling "Dammit, Louise, he's your son. I wish I had a son like that boy. Preston's father would never have allowed her to serve her son dead Blue Jays. I'm glad he can't see this."

I remember yelling at my mother, "I thought Uncle Virgil wanted them dead. He said he hated them."

My mother just looked at me, smiling in her mysterious way and said nothing.

"We left early the next morning with no breakfast and no goodbyes. Uncle Virgil came for a visit just before he died. The last we heard, Aunt was in a nursing home, somewhere outside of Atlanta. Years later, Judge Talley would learn that Junior Jackson was serving time for murder after shooting his second wife.

"Even after all these years, the roasted Blue Jays remain beyond explanation.

Somehow, I was supposed to understand the lesson of the unspoken rule about the dead Blue Jays, but I never did. Terrible things happen and are punished. We can't understand all the ways the world works. Love can be twisted into something else.

"Gradually, the terror of that visit with Uncle Virgil receded. I watched as my mother's beauty began to fade as she moved into her forties, and she became the office manager for the judge's thriving law practice. I thought maybe she was gathering evidence about the judge—not just his women but his favors and financial deals."

I finished my story about my mother and the Blue Jays, and then went back to my question about mistakes, deceptions, and betrayals. How I was never sure what the story really meant. And why my Mother kept such careful records about the judge.

Delores looked away.

"Perhaps she wanted the records to help her save you from the judge—if she ever needed to."

"Why would she need to?"

"You're very vulnerable."

"Who wouldn't be with my kind of childhood?"

Delores gave me a look that spoke of centuries of suffering, far worse than my own.

"Hmm. It's hard to put into words, but I think it's because of your face."

"My face?"

"Yes, I think so. Your face is very forgettable."

8.

I had left Bolivia and returned to Florida with the impossible idea of a meeting with Delores. I would win her over with my hope of our living together—somewhere and somehow.

I could reach her only through Ann Glazer, who was close to Delores. But Ann blocked all my efforts, saying that she had promised Delores not to reveal her whereabouts to anyone.

"What about Simon?" I asked.

Ann would only say that Simon's condition had worsened.

"Does that mean she will be leaving soon?"

Ann said Delores was conferring with doctors in Europe almost every day online.

I thought I was free and clear of Bolivia, and that terrifying chapter in my life: the times I was alone on the Itonomas River in a bateau with an old Johnson outboard, or after a drunken brawl I was caught up in with Chingo's pistol shots, or when I saw slaughtered cattle being packed with cocaine in the night, or when I was wading through an arroyo in the dark.

What I would later come to realize is that these events, by themselves, were trivial. If I concentrated on each of these individual incidents, they could begin to look like something devised by fate. King Momo, Delores's order not to come back, my old Florida friend Felix Guzman's advice to go far away—all these could be put together into something that resembled a plan—a criminal one. Was I delirious or gullible or willfully blind?

The next step seemed to be a move up the ladder of illusion, calling it necessity.

Countless circumstances began to weave a tapestry like the music of the metalcore band the Veil of Maya did for me. Maya, I had learned, was the attachment to the transitory components of our own experiences. The music of this band always drew this veil over me. What became important was not any detail in this veil of illusions but a sense of my own destiny. The entire phantom veil could vanish, taking with it all my dreams. My desperate efforts were to make sense of this veil before my death which, without Delores, could not come too soon.

But before this veil was lifted, I was summoned to the local F.B.I. office in Jacksonville with the approval of my boss at my law firm, Amaya Wheeler, an African-American woman with a sharp blonde haircut. She was a friend of Judge Talley's.

Because I had done such a good job with my first assignment at the firm, making a witness list for a murder trial, she had recommended that I be assigned to what was called the 'Bolivian Project.' I had to leave immediately as soon as I could.. Words like 'project' and 'assigned' predisposed me think of something like a rational plan. But there was no overall rational plan. All of the players involved, from Arturo Suárez to Ed Baker to me, Preston Ballard, had their own individual idea of what that 'rational plan' looked like.

I felt expendable, and so I agreed with a shrug, and said "Why not?"

Of course, this plan was communicated in generic code words that were really commands, like when I was told that this was a brief assignment that could be seen like a vacation, until I heard Amaya say, "We need you to be there right away."

I knew that Amaya Wheeler had agreed to this Bolivian Project behind my back, which was infuriating. I felt the hand of death on my shoulder, just as I would feel it later when I tried to pull an old aunt and her two nieces from an overturned oxcart at the bottom of a dry arroyo. I was told that the oxcart was not only the slowest way to travel but also the safest. All four of us on that slow trip were almost crushed to death. This was the vacation.

For some time, I had begun to suspect that Evaldo Hauser, my closest friend in law school, was somehow involved in his family's alliance with the Suárez drug trade. I had not wanted to believe this, but when I arrived in Magdalena, hoping that Evaldo would be waiting for me. I was to help take his father to Brazil. I found out that Evaldo was away in Cochabamba with his new mistress.

I would realize too late that it was not a cancer treatment that was needed for Evaldo's father, but it was money that was needed to develop a breed of cattle that could survive in the tropics and the only established available resource of money was Bolivian cocaine.

For centuries the Indians had grown cocaine, chewing on a wad of coca leaves to dull the pain of injuries or hard work. But the explosion of the market for refined cocaine, which magnified the effects of the drug into an addictive high, had exploded on the streets of America. This gave Evaldo the chance to make a fortune and save his family's sprawling forty thousand acres where large herds of cattle were grazing and dying from tropical diseases.

Other things gradually became clear. Evaldo's law degree offered him an opportunity to protect the inheritance left by his father, Don Eduardo, whose cancer was never mentioned after

I arrived. The cancer treatment had simply been almost falsehood—it was a checkup, but presented as a life and death one and it was meant to persuade me to come to Bolivia. So I was a guest, but with the secret assignment from my law office to write a report for the F.B.I. on the destinations for the shipments of Bolivian cocaine. Was I betraying my friend and his family? I was completely out of my element in every way with the Hausers. Bolivia was in a nightmare, and just barely survived. I would never go back.

And, since Delores had also ordered me not to return.

Amaya told me I had a new assignment in Savannah. All I knew about that old city was that the city had surrendered to Sherman, unlike Atlanta, and had saved itself from destruction. Surrendering to reality was what I needed to learn but could not.

Savannah was somehow connected to Bolivian cocaine production. I hoped this new assignment would not include another trip to Bolivia, but I still wanted to say no to going.

Amaya pointed out that my junior position at the law firm required me to do this follow-up in Savannah under the guidance and protection of the F.B.I. I was now, it seemed, "on loan" to the F.B.I. in another place.

Savannah had, I learned, become the port of choice for Bolivian cocaine shipments to the States.

I knew now that my hosts in Bolivia, were involved in this illegal drug trafficking.

The bloody carcasses of the cattle, filled with bags of cocaine paste, and loaded into a cargo plane in San Ramón was owned by the Suárez brothers, the only major Bolivian players.

The Hausers were, I guessed, were doing the hard work on the ground: buying the raw cocaine from local farms in the mountains, processing it in Beni, and then sending it to the States. But how?

At an even deeper level, I could hear King Momo's warning in Magdalena, echoing what Delores had said, "Don't come back."

I didn't know how these two things were connected: The Hausers' involvement with cocaine trafficking and the message sent from Delores via King Momo. I was convinced, however, that somehow there was a connection.

I knew that Evaldo's dream had been to develop a new breed of cattle that would be more resistant to infectious diseases than the local indigenous breeds. It seemed this dream had been connected to cocaine's promise of easy riches. Cocaine money could be used to turn Beni into a much-needed place for cattle ranches to thrive. It could fund projects to drain the annual flooding of the almost endless pampas or build secure road connections to Cochabamba and the major cities of La Paz and Sucre in the high altiplano of the Andes.

The trouble was that the Mexican cartels and the Suárezes did not share this dream. They wanted the money from the cocaine processed and shipped out. Who cared about cattle production when millions could be made shipping the magical white powder that was readily available?

Two days later, after the law firm had made clear my choices—go to Savannah or lose my job—I packed my bag and headed north to Savannah. I hoped to follow the trail of cocaine that might somehow might connect all the pieces–the Hausers and Delores and her warning not to come back.

In Savannah, I found myself waiting to meet the two Confidential Informants or C.I.'s that the F.B.I.'s Ed Baker had assigned to the project. I would be working with them. Before I met them, however, Agent Baker wanted a preliminary meeting with me so he could bring me up to speed on the situation in Savannah.

He recommended a new restaurant called Joelle's where we had some wine and talked before ordering. I tried to get some kind information about my new partners, but Ed just shrugged and said, "I'll let you make up your own mind." This sounded like the same casual 'Nothing to worry about' explanation I was given in Bolivia when crocodiles and piranhas were mentioned.

"Don't worry," Baker said, "I also have a real Bolivian on my payroll who will keep us up to date and give us the shipment information from San Ramón. You'll have three agents in Savannah assigned to you twenty-four/seven, so even when you are sight-seeing or having lunch at "Mother and Sons," my team will have your back.

"Let's make sure we all keep our phones on, night and day. We will all meet up at dinner tonight."

I filed this "real Bolivian" in the back of my mind, wondering who it was. I was almost sure it had to be Evaldo, and I made a bet with myself that he would not show up at the meeting. He was never where I expected him to be.

This plan of Ed Baker's reminded me of another time when "a real Bolivian" had not shown up, the time when I was watching with Chingo, and almost the entire village of San Ramón, as carcasses of recently slaughtered cattle packed with cocaine paste were loaded on a plane.

This promise of safety did not reassure me. In the last two months, I had read about Savannah's riverfront, lined with ships unloading smuggled drugs, and drenched in the blood from dead dealers and bystanders in one more recent confrontation.

I tried to tell Ed Baker about my fears.

"I've had too many 'reassuring promises' about safety recently, so I have my doubts."

Ed gave me a look and said, "Tell me about it."

"Do we have time?"

Ed started to answer, but his phone began to ring. He held up his hand and reached for it, listened for a moment and said "When?"

After another brief pause, he said "Good," and hung up.

"Your C.I.s are running late. So go ahead with your story. I'd like to hear it."

I was still not sure if Ed would understand. "

It's a long story," I said, "but it might throw some light on what I think the Hausers are planning."

"I'm a good listener," Ed answered.

I launched into my story of my dangerous journey in an oxcart, which Chingo had described as the world's safest mode of transportation.

It all started with Chingo's youngest sister Lina and her girlfriend Emilia. They were bored. They lived in Cochabamba where they were students at a Catholic boarding school for rich girls. They were staying with the Hausers in Magdalena for a long holiday and after a few days of small-town life in Magdalena, they were getting desperate for a change of scene. So Chingo suggested a visit to Irobi, one of his family's ranches.

He was sending an oxcart loaded with supplies, and they could ride along, together with their old aunt, nicknamed Tia ChaCha.

I would be the visiting Gringo who would keep them company. We would stay for a week or so, ride horses and paddle along the river looking for parrots.

I suspected that Irobi might be connected to the drug operation I had seen at San Ramón. The Hausers had started clearing land at Irobi for a small landing strip a few years ago. It was a slow process. They were still trying to complete it.

Chingo said he would be coming to Irobi a week later with a business friend who was interested in buying some cattle for crossbreeding purposes. The friend had a large two-engine passenger plane. Lena, Emilia, and I could fly back to Magdalena with Chingo and his friend, who piloted the plane.

Tia ChaCha wanted to stay at Irobi for a longer visit with Don Silas and his wife, Lola, who were her old friends. The women would have a room to themselves and sleep in hammocks, and I could string a hammock up on the front porch. Silas Gunther, the ranch foreman, was a man of about sixty, whose father had been a German refugee from WWII and would be on hand to help us with the horses, while Lola would do the cooking and cleaning. They would enjoy the company.

Tia ChaCha and the girls reluctantly agreed to fly back.

I would have done anything to relieve my hopelessness, my suicidal thoughts.

Not knowing what I was getting into and hoping as usual for an end-it-all accident, I said, "Let's go."

The problem was the oxcart, the slowest form of transportation on wheels. It is also, Chingo laughed, the safest, since "What could go wrong when you're moving at the speed of an overweight man?"

The oxcart was primitive, with two giant wooden wheels, and pulled by a team of four oxen. The wagon had been extended in the back and was partially filled with supplies needed at the ranch. There was not much to worry about driving the oxen.

They just plodded straight ahead.

"So, how long will the trip take?" I asked Chingo, thinking maybe four or five hours.

Chingo paused, squinted his eyes, and said, "Well, since we're not going to stop for anything, maybe twenty-four hours."

Seeing the stunned look, Chingo tried to reassure me. "Don't worry, you leave tomorrow at noon, travel through the cool of the night and pull into Irobi around noon the next day. It's the dry season, so no mosquitoes.

"It's an oxcart. You'll be safe. Avellino's been a driver since he was ten."

"How old is he now?"

"Maybe fourteen."

The next day after lunch, Tia ChaCha, Lina, Emilia, and I walked down to the river. Avellino was waiting with the loaded oxcart. I suspected that Irobi might be connected to the operation San Ramón.

The tank of gasoline was hanging off the back of the wagon. Tia ChaCha sat with her back against block of salt with a cow hide thrown over it. The two girls came next. I was up front with Avellino, who watched us position ourselves in the cart and then led the oxcart across the river and up the bank.

The pampas stretching for miles and miles, flat as a table and shining in the sun.

Avellino touched the back of the oxen with a small whip and the team lurched ahead pulling the wagon. We were slowly, slowly rolling forward.

At first the two girls and Tia ChaCha laughed and talked with one another. The wheels turned slowly with high screeching sounds that reminded me of where I was—in the middle of nowhere.

Agent Baker had said there were no laws to break in this empty sea of grass, but there would be plenty of arrests when "the product" reached Savannah.

Almost immediately things went wrong.

There was an irregular screech from the one of the wheels, which turned four of us into hypnotized zombies, listening, hunched over, trying to guess when the next

shriek of the wheel was coming, saying things like "Here it comes," or "Get ready."

After another hour or so, Tia ChaCha yelled, "Avellino, for the love of God, stop and put some grease on that wheel!"

Avellino said, "Grease? There is no grease, Señora."

And so we creaked on. The sun dropped lower in the sky, and spotted a small grove of trees.

Tia ChaCha yelled, "Avellino, stop at those trees up ahead. We need to relieve ourselves."

Avellino jumped off the wagon and guided the oxen over to the grove of trees.

Tia ChaCha and the two girls came tumbling out and disappeared. I waited until they came back and then hurried into the trees. As I headed back, I could see they had spread out our supper on the back of the oxcart.

This was our big meal until noon the next day. In Beni, beef was an everyday item, so we had a welcome change: baked chicken and rice, with a surprise, a custard flan. Tomorrow would be charque or strips of dried beef. If all went well, we would reach Irobi by noon the next day.

Lina and Emilia began moaning about not being able to take a bath, but Tia ChaCha gave them a look and they stopped the whining.

Even after Avellino had finished eating there were still two pieces of chicken left.

As Tia ChaCha started to put the chicken away when Avellino came over began whispering to Tia Chacha, Avellino pointing to the squeaky wheel and Tia ChaCha nodding.

After a moment, they stopped and Tia ChaCha looked at us, then pointed to Avellino.

"He's going to fix the wheel."

Taking a mallet, Tia ChaCha began pounding the pieces of leftover chicken.

Then Avellino used the mallet to loosen the wheel from the axle just enough so he could squeeze in the greasy chicken around the axle with his knife. Using the mallet again, Avellino tightened the wheel around the axle greased by the chicken.

We got back in the wagon; the girls began applauding Avellino and Tia ChaCha's ingenuity.

Off we rolled. There were no shrieks from the wheel, and we all congratulated Avellino.

In another hour it was dark. The sky was clear, so there was enough starlight out in the open pampas to see anything dangerous in front of us. In a couple of hours a half-moon came up over the horizon with enough light to turn the pampas into a silver sea.

Soon, Tia ChaCha and the girls were sleeping, curled up in the back into a jumbled knot of arms and legs.

I stayed awake, wondering if I would get closer to the source of the Hausers' plans at Irobi. Had they developed a route to bypass Mexico, and secure their own shipments of cocaine?

The pampas were hardly a smooth highway, and the oxcart had hit every ditch.

Every so often I would say "Avellino?" and he would reply "Está bien, Señor."

Then, I would drift off into half sleep only to wake up and see Avellino, on the front seat, with his head swaying back and forth as the oxcart slowly moved through the endless sea of grass like a large ship leaving no wake. I remember thinking What could go wrong? It's an oxcart, and then falling back to sleep.

Then I was wide awake.

I could hear Avellino yelling.

I felt I was being hurled through the air until I hit the ground hard enough to knock the wind out of me, and Avellino was bending over and shaking me, saying "¡Señor!¡ Señor!" over and over again.

Evidently, Avellino had fallen asleep on the front seat. When we reached the dry bed of the arroyo, without Avellino's guidance, the oxen had started down the steep bank. Pushed by the heavy weight of the oxcart behind them, the two lead oxen began wildly running faster and faster. But, blocked by the high bank of the arroyo on other side, they were forced to do a hard right, pitching the oxcart over.

They would have gone on running down the dry bed of the arroyo that stretched in front them like an open road, but Avellino, who had been thrown clear, had jumped out in front of the oxen, and they stopped just in time not to kill the fourteen-year-old boy.

After he unhitched their harness and removed their heavy wooden yokes, he came over to check on me as I struggled to stand up. Then he led me over to the oxen with the unnecessary instructions.

"Cuidado, be careful, and stay in front of them." The oxen, being docile beasts, let me live.

Back at the overturned oxcart, the real miracle was that Tia ChaCha, Lina and Emilia were not hurt, though bruised and sore. Tia ChaCha was still pinned under the cart with the girls, but she calmly talked Avellino through how to pull her and the girls out through the front of the oxcart.

The gasoline tank on the back of the oxcart had been secured well enough to withstand the shock of the overturned cart. If the tank had broken loose, or if the oxen had not been stopped by Avellino and had continued dragging the cart, there would have been broken bones, and someone would surely have been crushed. No one ever talked about the danger. I tried to use the no talking lesson about Delores—no thinking about her either!

So much for my safe trip!

As it was, we all found ourselves standing next to the upended oxcart. The moon was out. It was Tia ChaCha who took charge. She pointed to Avellino, who would have to save us again.

"How?" I wondered. In any direction help was miles away.

"Can you find Irobi?" Tia ChaCha asked him.

"I have been there many times, Señora."

"Good, Avellino," she said. "You'll have to go on foot. Find Don Silas. Tell him what happened and where we are. He should send a rider and four horses, plus enough men to get the oxcart up off its side, so the gasoline, rope and salt can come with us in the oxcart to Irobi."

Avellino listened. "I understand, Señora, but it will take time."

Tia ChaCha smiled. "We're not going anywhere."

Avellino turned to go but was stopped by Tia ChaCha.

"There's a small bottle of water in the oxcart. Take it with you." Avellino took the bottle, and we watched as he climbed the bank of the arroyo and disappeared. As we stood there, I felt the isolation and danger, but there were no thoughts of Delores.

"How far is it to Irobi?" I asked Tia ChaCha.

She waited, and then said, "It's hard to say. It's been a long time since I was out here. Traveling by oxcart throws off my sense of time. I'm guessing that we were about halfway to Irobi when we turned over, so Avellino should be there around noon.

Don Silas will send help, so maybe by sundown tomorrow we will have some company."

The light from the moon disappeared. We waited in the dark, alert for any sounds of animals around us. The oxen knelt down and were quiet. The two girls huddled around Tia ChaCha and the three of them went to sleep.

I remembered that yesterday we had not seen any riders in the distance traveling through the pampas, not even a solitary traveler. We could only hope.

I had heard that the leopards had mostly been hunted out, and that there were some poisonous snakes, but that they usually avoided humans.

What about Avellino? Could he make it to Irobi on foot? Was he barefoot or wearing sandals? Why didn't I volunteer to go with him? Then I thought that was stupid, since I probably would not have made it.

We waited for hours. I fell asleep on my side. When I opened my eyes I could see the faintest glimmer of light over the rim of the arroyo. The oxen began shifting around. Tia ChaCha woke up. I waved and she waved back, then she pointed to the wagon and made eating gestures. I went over to the wagon and found the small burlap bags with our food. There was one bottle of water.

The girls woke up. We chewed on the dried charque and took little sips of the water.

About every five minutes one of girls would ask "How much longer?" We went on like this until the sun reached its zenith.

When Lina asked that question perhaps for the hundredth time, Tia ChaCha looked up at the sun and said, "Avellino should be at Irobi about now."

I put my head down and thought It's going to be another long, long wait.

But I was wrong. An hour later we could hear horses, and a man yelling.

Chingo, we later learned, had sent a rider to Irobi the day before we left Magdalena, alerting the foreman, Don Silas that we were leaving the next day. Don Silas, knowing that we were coming in an oxcart, had come out to meet us, bringing a string of four horses. He had met Avellino heading for Irobi, and the two of them rode back to find us. The oxcart could not be easily repaired, so Avellino was given a horse and told to take the oxen back to Magdalena.

Soon we were riding back to Irobi with the two girls doubling up on one horse.

Four hours later, we were eating the hot steak, platino, beans and rice that Señora Lola had waiting for us.

We were alive! I could concentrate on that and not on the Hausers, the Suárezes, the F.B.I., not even on Delores.

I looked at Ed Baker who was leaning forward and went on.

"I never heard what happened to the gasoline, salt, and rope we were carrying, but that trip in an oxcart was the closest brush with death I've ever had. So maybe you can understand why I don't trust anyone who, in an obviously dangerous situation, keeps telling me not to worry. Or that, riding in an oxcart is the safest form of travel."

I tried to read his mind. Like the F.B.I. man he was, he picked up on the one piece of information I had forgotten to include.

"So, what happened after you reached the Irobi? Did you learn anything new about the Hausers' efforts to develop their own independent connections to the cocaine market to the States without the Mexican Suárezes?"

"Yes, while in Irobi, I went out for a ride with Don Silas. I learned that the small runway is being lengthened."

Suddenly alert, Agent Baker leaned forward. "How long has this been going on?"

"About five or six years. A small tribe of Indians has been clearing out the big trees, using axes, shovels, and picks to take them down, dig up the big roots and clear out the limbs. It's incredibly slow work that can be done only in the dry season. The Indians only stay for a couple of months and then move down the rivers looking for more work. Don Silas estimated that it would take five or six more years before the runway was ready."

Agent Baker nodded his head. "So, the gasoline in the oxcart was for...?"

"The Hausers have a small bulldozer waiting on the Brazilian border at Guayaramerín. When the rains come, they'll put the dozer on a barge and tow it down the Mamore via the Itonomas to Irobi. If that works out, the runway will be ready this time next year."

"Bulldozers run on diesel fuel."

Agent Baker was right, but it didn't matter. In the Beni, gasoline and diesel fuel were always needed. I shrugged, and said

"When the time comes, I'm sure they will have diesel fuel to run the bulldozer."

"What would that mean?"

"A conservative estimate would double their cocaine production. And if the Hausers buy even a small cargo plane, it might double again."

I paused and added, "Maybe. Remember, in the Beni there's no electricity except from generators. No roads and no gas station to fill up the tank. No supplies to replace broken tools and parts.

I don't know if the Hausers have enough money for that. Right now, they still depend on the Suárez brothers to fly in needed supplies and fly out the cocaine." I was thinking about Evaldo.

"And?" Ed asked, waiting for me to go on.

"Evaldo would sometimes talk about saving the ranches, meaning the cattle herds his father had established. The only way to do that will be with the help of cash from the booming cocaine market. It's still legal to grow coca in Bolivia."

Baker shifted in his chair.

"Then, the next step is the Suárez brothers, who are almost set in Savannah.

They will want to cut out your friends, the Hausers, who will, I am sure, end up with the short end of the stick. It is Mexico that stands in the way. It blocks the route for the Bolivian cocaine on the way to the States with the help of the Suárezes."

"I'll bet on the Hausers," I said out of blind loyalty, remembering Evaldo's skills to maneuver his projects and ingratiate himself with powerful people.

Baker leaned back in his chair. "If you're right, I'll buy you a steak at Tom Sarris's Steak House in D.C. when all of this is over."

9.

We waited at Joelle's for a couple of minutes, looking at the menu and taking sips of wine when Ed gave me a look and pointed to the lobby.

"Here come your C. I.s, Queenie, and Charley."

They moved with ease through the room, almost bouncing with each step. They were dressed from consignment shops like graduate students. Ed introduced me simply as 'Your Contact' and then he left, leaving me sitting at the table and wondering how to begin.

Queenie smiled and picked up her menu, then said, "I am totally starved."

"I'm a stranger in town, so tell me what's good. Uncle Sam is paying."

They recommended a Low Country Boil of shrimp and grits with ice cold beer, followed by a slice of cake and coffee.

We took our time.

They asked, "How was your trip?"

I asked, "How long have you been in Savannah?"

We continued like this for a few more minutes and, thinking I had waited long enough, I asked, "So, what else do you guys do?"

They exchanged looks. Queenie pointed at me and in a stage whisper to Charley said, "He doesn't know!"

Then they jumped up and did a silent routine about a man propositioning a woman on the street. He makes a move and she rebuffs him, all the while miming their talk while making me perfectly understand what was happening, all without words. By then, the entire dining room was watching and yelling encouragement until a drunk man in a Brooks Brothers sport coat—I knew a Brooks Brothers when I saw one because the judge had several—stood up.

Holding on to his chair began bellowing, "What the fuck?! I need another drink and where the hell is my dinner."

Queenie and Charley slipped behind me, and I walked up to the drunk and said in his face, "Sit down now, Sir. Do not say another word!"

I had never done such a thing, even when the judge had insulted my mother.

"We're mimes!" Queenie and Charley bowed from behind my back and then slid into their seats.

The room had fallen under their spell, and I stood up again and shouted, "So what do you say, folks. Let's give them a hand."

There were cheers and applause. Queenie and Charley jumped up, fully recovered from the heckler's attack. They raised their arms in thanks to the other diners and strutted around the tables, like the leaders of a marching band.

We finished our meal and agreed to meet at Oglethorpe Square the next day at noon, where I could catch their regular act. Afterwards we would meet again with Ed Baker and find out what the F.B.I. wanted us to do.

They were certainly not what I expected, not in a million years. I gave them a ride to their apartment in my rented car and we said goodnight.

I drove back to my hotel, miserable and depressed, bewildered by the surreal dinner at Joelle's with Queenie and Charley which brought back the nightmare of my time in Bolivia—the bats, heads of dead cattle, eyes glittering in the firelight, King Momo's repeating Delores'scruel command "Don't come back."

Alone and needing comfort, I confronted the soullessness of my hotel room.

There was a little note from the management about how "special" I was, followed by checkout times and info about paying bills.

I undressed, took a shower and slipped into a pair of pajamas I had left out on the bed, now icy cold from the extreme A.C. A mini-refrigerator tucked in a corner was stocked with mini-bottles of vodka and bourbon. A shower that needed help.

I felt that I was in deeper shit than ever. Even deeper than in Bolivia. Turning over in the oxcart or on the Itonomas alone, and finding my way back to Magdalena.

I poured a hefty shot of Makers Mark into a plastic glass, added some mini-ice cubes, and tap water. Then I turned down the A.C. and stretched out on the bed.

It was now time for other thoughts, which were followed by extreme regret seasoned with a heavy dose of anger: Who was I kidding? Mimes as Confidential Informants? An F.B.I. agent who offered no real explanation of what I would be doing.

Betrayed by my law firm about Bolivia, and now again in Savannah.

I was working with smoke and mirrors with the help of mimes! Not to mention, the married woman I loved who told me to never come back, and who often reminded me that I had a very forgettable face, even after we'd had great sex.

And what Ed Baker had said, in a casual way, about a Bolivian who had our cell phone numbers, and who was going to advise us about cargo ships bringing drugs to Savannah. Could he in fact be Evaldo Hauser, my law school friend, the man who was often not where he said he would be? Was he the "real Bolivian" who had not shown up at Joelle's the night before when Ed Baker expected him to come and be introduced?

Was it possible that, from the beginning, Evaldo had a more central role in this F.B.I. investigation? But why was I kept in the dark? I tried to understand the possible routes drugs might take to circumvent the old route through Mexico into the States, a new route that would, for the Hauser family, become the Silk Road bringing in the money to fund their dreams?

By my third round of Makers Mark, I was losing that moment of clarity about the threads I was following.

The judge always said, as the wine flowed, "In vino veritas." But the truth was too clouded.

I turned over and stopped trying. I could feel my muscles relax, and my angry questioning slide into It is what it is, and What the hell. Things will work out somehow, won't they?

I remembered a phrase from law school called Occam's razor: The simplest explanation is usually right. Delores had just been having a bad day when she told me "Don't come back." Evaldo was, in fact, my good friend who had invited me to visit his family in Bolivia. The mimes were brilliant readers of human nature and would silently find out where each ship with drugs would be unloading.

Finally, I fell into a drunken sleep, where the dreams of Delores felt like the real Delores in my arms and the ships with the drugs were lost in a storm at sea. Everyone was safe.

****

The next morning started with a brief rain shower followed by the sun glistening on the water drops still clinging to the grass.

I was sitting on a park bench in Oglethorpe Square waiting for Ed Baker, who would be coming with the long-promised no–show Bolivian, who would have some vital new information about the new route bypassing Mexico for shipping cocaine from Beni.

Queenie and Charley, my two recently acquired partners, were performing their street act.

Agent Baker had told me they were experts on the internet and knew all about how to find shipping schedules, dock security plans and safe contacts. At the same time, over the last six months, they had developed an informal network of informants "out on the street" as they put it.

Agent Baker said that in many ways, this allowed Queenie and Charley to come up with word-of-mouth information that more traditional informants would miss. Agent Baker was "constantly amazed" at how accurate some of their information was. "Don't let the clown suits fool you. They are really sharp operators."

Their routine featured a beggar and his companion. Charley placed a basket on the sidewalk and as people passed, he played a harmonica while Queenie sang in a frail voice filled with joy and sorrow, country songs like "Down in the Valley," and "When the Roll is Called Up Yonder."

Once a crowd had gathered, Charley explained that Queenie, who was introduced as The Incredible Twisted Lady, had been jilted at the altar, and was now afflicted by some kind of tropical bug that was like arthritis but worse, and that it had turned her body into a pretzel. At the same time, Charley walked in front of the crowd, tapping his cane on the sidewalk and pointing to a basket, while asking for a donation to help 'his sister'.

The 'reveal' came when the basket was full of money. Charley suddenly held up a blanket and Queenie stepped behind it. Then, in a flourish of the blanket, they emerged as preppies working as summer interns. They then sauntered away with the money while shaking their fingers and wagging their asses at the crowd.

But, to keep it all legal, they then stopped, and with sorrowful looks, came back, holding out the basket filled with the money for people to take back their donations. Of course, the crowd let them keep the money.

I learned that Queenie and Charley, as licensed street actors, would be my eyes and ears on the dangerous Savannah docks where drug raids happened regularly. I never knew their real names, but they reminded me of "Bubbles" in The Wire.

Watching them made me recall Carnival in Magdalena and the terrifying figure of King Mom when he had warned me of the threat waiting for me back in the States, while repeating verbatim Delores's warning— "Don't come back."

The old Savannah where Queenie and Charley were working, was laid out around large squares. On River Street, the waterfront district of mansions, restaurants, and antique shops, I sat and watched the large ocean-going vessels, some with foreign flags flying, maneuver the narrow channel as they headed out to the ocean.

Now, here I was, thinking I would be free of entanglements and that I had finally left the Bolivian assignment behind me forever. Instead, I found myself becoming even more deeply involved in it.

My law firm had secretly "loaned me" to the F.B.I. to find out how serious the reports were about the increase in Bolivian cocaine shipments. I hated my suspicions about my friend Evaldo and his family, who had been so hospitable, but maybe, I naively thought, they were afraid of Arturo and Hernando Suárez.

That was the only thing that could have led them to smuggling cocaine, so I had begun to suspect that the Hausers, my hosts, were involved, at some level, in this business, even at a higher level than the bloody carcasses of the cattle filled with bags of cocaine paste.

I was to report, with the help of Queenie and Charley, on the route for the cocaine, which would bypass Mexico by removing the packets of cocaine in La Paz and flying them to Cartagena on the Colombian coast, where they would be loaded onto a large ocean-going fishing trawler which would work its way northward to Tybee Island off the coast of Savannah.

From there the drugs would be off-loaded and transported down to Florida and Blue Palm Island. The F.B.I. wanted to know if the cocaine shipment was actually under way and exactly what the schedule was.

The F.B.I. had put this route together using information from several sources, including my own contribution, which I hoped was reliable and maybe the nail in the coffin of the case that the F.B.I. was putting together. Someone had pointed out that the trip from Cartagena to Florida by fishing trawler would take too long, and it was hoped that Queenie, Charley, and I could find out what the final schedule of the shipping route would be.

Agent Baker had sent a message saying we had an appointment with a man who had information about the Bolivian drug trade. I had been chosen for this Savannah mission because I had recently returned from Bolivia and had actually witnessed the start of the drug production there in Beni.

We would learn later from the F.B.I. that the secret source of information about Bolivian cocaine came with impressive clearance from someone in the high office in Washington. No one seemed to know exactly what this was all about, but we were to meet with the F.B.I. and their contact at the "Midnight in the Garden of Good and Evil" graveyard. I had liked the bestselling book, but I wasn't sure why this particular spot had been chosen.

Queenie laughed and said that there was no actual 'Good and Evil' graveyard.

Several of the parks in Savannah had been used as sites for the movie. "In Savannah," she said, "there's no garden, not much good, and lots of evil."

"So exactly where are we going?" I asked.

It was Charley who knew where we would meet our contact.

"We'll be there in about half an hour."

To pass they told stories about living in New York and attending the American Academy of Theatrical Arts. They were drawn to the Mime classes, where the first thing the famous mime teacher said, after a dramatic pause, was "Remember, Mimes can't talk."

"Maybe mimes live in the non-existent gardens where Bolivians never show up," I added.

"Exactly!" Queenie shouted.

We were all silent for a moment.

Charley asked, "What about Bolivia? Ed said you had been there."

"That's true."

"What if I said I wanted to take a trip to Bolivia? What would you say?"

"I would say, 'Don't go.'"

My answer seemed to put a damper on their questions about Bolivia. Things were quiet for a moment, and then Queenie grabbed Charley's arm. "Wait a minute! Do you remember that big party in Virginia?"

Charley wasn't sure.

"You remember, it was out in horse country. Lucie Freemont, the rich lady, hired us to entertain at her party."

"And...?" Charley added.

"It was weird.

"Lucie had rented a big bus to carry all of her guests from D.C. to the party at that enormous house she owned in the Virginia hunt country. We were in the back of the bus and were supposed to be the after-dinner entertainment, with a few magic tricks and mind readings.

"When we got to Lucie's estate nobody was around. All of the horses had been let out and were grazing in a field on the other side of a small stream. I think there was some misunderstanding about what day we were supposed to arrive. Anyway, we got off the bus and just stood there, not knowing what to do.

"And then one of the guests, this really good-looking guy, saddled the one horse left in the barn. He rode across the stream, rounded up the other horses and brought them back in."

Charley's memory seemed to kick in. "Yeah, O. K. But, so what?"

"I bet it's that guy who was at the party, the one who brought the horses in. I remember Lucie saying that he was from Bolivia."

I froze, thinking it could only be one person. "What was his name?"

Queenie was silent for a moment and then shook her head. "I can't remember. I know Lucie said his name, but I've forgotten. It was just that one time."

"Was it Evaldo Hauser?"

Queenie paused and then nodded.

"Yeah, that's it. It was Evaldo Hauser. I remember thinking I had never known anyone named Evaldo. I'm sure that he and Lucie were a pair for a while, but I guess it didn't work out, because she married some other guy a few months later. Anyway, it was a great party."

"I thought so too," I said.

"You were there?" Queenie asked shocked.

"Just briefly'" I said, enjoying Queenie's stunned look. "I had stayed around for a drink and then went back to D. C. on the bus. Evaldo and I were in law school together."

Queenie continued giving me a once over.

"I can't believe I don't remember you. I'm really good with faces."

"I've been told my face isn't memorable. In fact, I think the word used was 'forgettable.'

Queenie gave me an appraising look and said "Well, whoever told you that got it right."

"Thanks." I winced.

"What I mean is, I'm a mime. I study faces. I'm not sure how I would characterize yours. You look different every time I see you."

There was a pause, and Queenie, wanting to know more, asked "What were you doing in Bolivia?"

Before I could answer, Charley broke in.

"I think we're almost there."

The car slowed down and stopped where an old pier disappeared into what seemed like a sea of grassy islands, with glittering channels of water cutting through them in large, looping circles. There was a half-moon.

Charley said, "We're at an old bridge that crosses over the marshes on the Savannah near Tybee Island. Not many people know about this road."

We walked out to the end of a pier and waited, not sure what to do. Then not far away, there was the deep cough of a motor starting. Running lights came on, and we could see the outline of a small fishing boat as it nosed out from behind a small island of marsh grass about fifty yards from the end of the pier. It stopped, the motor idling.

The silhouette of a man appeared. A searchlight on the boat flashed on, illuminating us. The man stood watching us through a pair of binoculars. Then, another man appeared. Charley had a pair of binoculars and cried out "It's the Lady Lulu. I've boarded her several times when I've been on the Coast Guard patrol."

I stood watching as the Lady Lulu made her way through the winding channels of the marshes. The men were still standing in the stern, looking back at us.

As The Lady Lulu receded, I was certain one man was still watching us through binoculars. Just from the dark profile and the way he kept his balance in the speeding bateau, I knew it was Evaldo.

I lifted my arm, not in a salute, but a silent acknowledgement, as if to say, 'I know who you are.' I thought he might make some sign of acknowledgement, but then he turned away and disappeared inside the cabin.

During our ride home, Charley and Queenie talked in whispers about what we had seen and the mystery of it. "Why had they sent word for us to meet them?"

"They were looking for me." I said. I didn't explain that I knew Evaldo would want to make sure where I was, either in Savannah or on Blue Palm Island. Now he knew.

Was he waiting for me, looking for me or hunting me?

I could tell that Queenie and Charley wanted to draw me out; to make sure they knew whose side I was on before that first shipment of cocaine came in. I didn't mention that I was almost certain that I had recognized Evaldo Hauser. Back in my motel room, I hit the Makers Mark again and fell asleep.

****

The next morning, I reported my take on what I thought had happened out in the marshes the night before. Baker listened and said, "That's what I thought you would find. Give me a day to put all of this in my report." He then added, "You can take the day off and enjoy Savannah."

An hour later I was breaking all speed limits on my way back to the Blue Palm. I had just a few hours to learn more about Delores. Could I break through that protective wall of silence she had built around herself?

All I had was our words. I had no tangible token that lovers usually have, no note promising to meet again, no love gift to cherish. Our one meeting place, the Far Cottage, was now like a dream.

I knew that Simon would always be in front of me. What I could not understand was why Delores refused to include me in the future. I had told her that I would wait. All I received in return was the command "Don't come back."

And then I thought, perhaps I had said too much. Perhaps those stories at the Far Cottage were too revealing, and that the story of my childhood and my mother's cruelty had shown her nothing more than my weakness. Someone who would not be able to stand with her against the combined forces of our pasts? My doubts and fears swirled about me, which was exactly what I didn't need.

I needed to find Delores.

If it was goodbye, or wait until later, or meet me in Switzerland, or whatever, we needed to talk. But no matter what she said or did, I just needed to see her.

As I reached the bridge to the Blue Palm Island, I slowed the car down and then stopped, trying to orient myself.

I was like someone who comes to a place he has known all of his life, only to find it totally changed. The old bridge with its plank boards covered with tar paper was gone and in its place was a new bridge that, I am sure, was designed to look as if it had always been there.

I walked out to the middle span where a new wooden trellis was supported by steel pilings. I looked over the railings to see where Ann Glazer and I would come after we had practiced our water-skiing routines, at the point below the bridge where the black water of the Ogeechee flows into the ocean. It now seemed a thousand years ago.

I remembered trying to persuade Sandy Lefcourt, the manager of the Blue Palm, to repair the bridge. Every week trucks bringing supplies for the hotel rolled over it.

Judge Talley once warned Lefcourt that it was a wonder that a bus filled with rich investors and tourists hadn't gone into the Ogeechee. The new bridge was a good omen.

As I drove through the grounds leading up to the hotel, I saw a sign that said that the hotel was closed for restorations.

I parked and headed down the broad walkway that led to the front entrance. As I reached the steps, Sandy Lefcourt came out. We both stopped, then he smiled and waved.

"Hello Preston. It's been a while."

I wasn't sure if he knew about my trip to Bolivia. "I've been away for several months. I've finished law school and I'm working in Daytona. I wanted to visit my mother, and someone told me she and Judge Talley might be here for a get together with friends."

"I haven't seen your mother recently. Judge Talley left a couple of hours ago. He was in a meeting with Mr. Khumar all morning."

I wanted to turn the conversation to Delores, but wasn't sure how, so I tried a straightforward, "Is Mrs. Khumar here?"

Lefcourt was immediately on guard. "Yes, I believe she is. I'm going up to join them. Can I give her a message?"

"Yes, please tell her I did come back." Lefcourt looked puzzled, so I added, "She'll understand."

Lefcourt nodded, and then said, "Did you notice the improvements on the Island Bridge?"

"I did. I stopped and looked around. It's really impressive."

"I thought a new bridge would be a major improvement, and Mr. Khumar finally agreed. I'm glad it's finished."

"I'm glad you changed his mind. Sooner or later that old bridge would have collapsed."

"Mr. Khumar doesn't like change," Lefcourt added.

I turned to go, but Lefcourt stopped me.

"I guess you saw there were no guests around. We're doing major renovations to the hotel and the grounds. We've shut things down for a month until all the work inside is finished. Mrs. Khumar put together a new art collection that will be in the lobby.

We're planning a gala celebration when it's all completed."

I wanted to ask more about Delores, but her last words as I left the Far Cottage stopped me.

Instead I asked, "Do you ever see Ann Glazer? Wasn't she finishing her last year of nursing school?"

Lefcourt looked surprised. "Why do you ask?"

"She was a good friend in high school. She was working here the summer after we graduated. She recommended me for my first job here."

"Of course. I remember that, now. She gave you a glowing recommendation."

"I've been away for a while and thought I would look her up."

Lefcourt smiled. "Well, you won't have far to go. She's helping me organize the gala. We turned the Far Cottage into her office."

I tried to hide my surprise, and only said, "I'll have to drop by and say hello."

"She would love to see you. You've been away, so of course you don't know.

Ann is Mrs. Lefcourt now. We're married. You were in Bolivia at the time. Ann wanted to send you an invitation, but…" his voice trailed off.

I extended my hand.

"Congratulations. You're a lucky man."

"We've kept it quiet. The Khumars renovated a suite on the top floor for us as a wedding present. I signed a long-term contract to manage the hotel and Ann will take care of the guests and event planning."

"The Khumars are lucky to have you both."

Lefcourt gave me a concerned look, as if hesitating to say something.

"I should tell you that Mr. Khumar's condition is much worse. The doctors say he will need long-term care. He wants to go back to Europe, and I think Mrs. Khumar has arranged to move him to a sanitarium in Switzerland.

"We're not sure of the exact date, but they will be leaving very soon, maybe in the next day or two. That's what I meant earlier about his hating changes.

"If you see Ann or Mrs. Khumar they might bring these things up, but please don't mention these plans to anyone."

"Of course not."

"Oh, and one more thing. Judge Talley is helping with some legal issues before they leave..." His voice trailed off.

I was desperate to ask about Delores but sensed that this wasn't the time.

Lefcourt obviously didn't want to keep the conversation going, so I just extended my hand again, and said, "I know you and Ann will be happy," and turned to leave.

I walked toward my car, blinded by the sun, and trying to take in the idea of Delores caring for Khumar in Switzerland.

Lefcourt had said they were leaving in the next day or two, so I didn't have much time to find her. Her old cell number, the one I had tried many times in Bolivia, was no longer working.

As I reached for my keys, a thought seemed to come out of nowhere, and shattered all my old ideas of what was happening. Could it be that the last day I saw Delores before leaving for Bolivia, the day she said 'Don't come back,' she already knew she would be leaving and that she had already made the plan to leave?

She knew when she warned me not to come back that she would not be at the Blue Palm, and she was trying to tell me this; not a goodbye, as I had thought, but that she would not be at the Blue Palm when I came back from Bolivia. She was leaving it up to me, I could follow her to Switzerland or stay here; it would be my choice.

I had to believe that she wanted me to follow her, and I already knew in my heart that I would. Only one thing made me hesitate; Delores was still here. Had I come back earlier than she expected? Or, had her plans changed in some way that she hadn't foreseen? I only knew that I did not have much time.

I started my car and headed back across the new bridge, wildly alive to the hope that was spinning endless possibilities of what I could do. Delores had not been able to leave quickly enough to avoid me, I thought, and now I was back and there was a chance that somehow. We could start our lives together, here or in Switzerland. She was not deserting her husband but going with him.

After my conversation with Lefcourt, I realized how out of touch I was. The only family we had left was my father's older brother, my Uncle Virgil who survived landing on Omaha beach with boats loaded with tons of ammunition.

It was in Clover, Florida where the judge saw my mother as his mistress, and my mother saw him as a way to pay for my college and law school. This was a double bind, not only for her but for me.

Later, he would get me into law school and then secure an entry level position at Benson & Jones, where one of his women Amaya Wheeler, was a partner and would be the one who would send me to Bolivia. It seemed that my life could be described as a series of landings. Ones that I had no control over—of being "hurled, headlong flaming," like Milton's Lucifer's leaving heaven– things happened to me and I had to deal with them.

Clover was a small Florida town when I was growing up, but now, it had become a part of what was called the "Greater Jacksonville-Palatka loop," which included the St. Johns River. As kids, we called it "Lackawanna" because it seemed to lack almost everything we wanted.

Tucked away on a small off-shore Island connected by an old bridge to the mainland, the Blue Palm was seen as an out-of-date relic from the early twenties. Most of the small business appeared and then disappeared overnight. The flocks of tourists had moved to the flashier Florida from Palm Beach to Miami.

My first summer job in high school was at one of the 'Big Orange' stands that were found everywhere in Florida, along with their signs reminding you "Only two more miles to the next Big Orange." As the 'Assistant Manager' my job was—guess what?

Squeezing an endless supply of big oranges.

At Clover High, I longed to be in a world of doors opening out to other places. I fell in love with the poetry of Phillip Larkin, who wrote of such things: the despair of those longing to make a new start, and the risk of doing so. When I was younger, his line, "And then she undid her dress" gave me chills.

I had always envied people who risked all and made a new start. Yet I remained torn between Larkin's "...then she undid her dress" and Housman's "It rains into the sea/And still the sea is salt."

Breaking free had always seemed impossible until I met Delores. If only I could find her, and soon.

I needed to meet with Ed Baker and find out if he had located Evaldo. How would I tell him I might be leaving for Europe? The F.B.I. no longer needed me as they planned their moves against the major players in this newly formed Bolivian enterprise. I didn't want to be around when they brought the drugs in to Savannah. Above all, I didn't want to be in court to testify against the people I had known in the Beni; the people I had deceived, my hosts and friends.

What would a new life mean? I was never good at thinking about the future, never able to direct my own actions, but only to react to other people's plans as they tried to fit me into their designs. I would have to survive wherever I landed. With Delores I would have the gift of love and freedom I needed.

Would she let me go with her, stay with her, run away to live with her somewhere we had not yet heard of? Or maybe Switzerland, as companions to Khumar until he died.

11.

As I left the Blue Palm I tried to think about how to tell Agent Baker that my assignment with the F.B.I. was over.

Bolivia had almost killed me, and I wanted out. I needed to leave before the drugs from Bolivia arrived at an undesignated port, as far as I knew. It was only five more miles to the F.B.I. office, and I still did not have an exit plan for resigning.

I knew that Amaya Wheeler, the junior partner, had given me a renewal contract, which was a way of saying I could be let go at any time. But I would insist that it also could mean that I had the right to leave when I wanted to.

I knew she wanted the law office to get credit for assisting the F.B.I. in its efforts to interrupt the drug traffic from South America to the States. But I was through.

Good luck, I thought. I had my own life to deal with, convincing Delores that I was not going away.

I thought about Tybee Island as a possible destination for the Bolivian drugs I had seen packed in the carcasses of Chingo's cattle. I knew Tybee was just beginning to become part of the huge flow of drugs coming into the States from the south.

I was sure that Agent Baker had a plan for using me in the Savannah/Tybee drug raid. Tybee had seemed an unlikely place—with its family vacation homes and theater, T-shirts and surfboard shops, plus a famous old lighthouse. But maybe that ordinariness made it a good place for drug deliveries.

How would I tell the formidable Amaya Wheeler that I was jumping ship from this project? And I knew I had to make Agent Baker release me from my role as an untrained but paid informant?

I was suddenly exhilarated by thinking of the moment I would say to Ed Baker 'No, I have other plans.' Then he would ask 'Other plans for what?' and I would be silenced, as usual. But I would be free to track down Delores.

Agent Baker was probably in Savannah meeting with the two mimes/Confidential Informants about the twilight sighting of the Evaldo Hauser figure in the fishing boat near Tybee Island. The whole business was beginning to remind me of The Bourne Identity movie, except that Charley, Queenie, and yours truly, were chasing people with real guns.

I was a cheap version of Hamlet, someone unable to "take arms against a sea of troubles."

I kept telling myself that somewhere out there in F.B.I. Land people like Agent Baker could see the 'Big Picture' and know that I was just a small part of it. Only an extra in the crowd, waiting to be cut from the payroll when I was no longer needed.

This was what I believed, but as I walked into the F.B.I.'s satellite office and gave my name to the intern at the reception desk my confidence ebbed. Even lower when, after checking her list of appointments, she looked up and said, "Sorry, but I don't see your name."

"I've been working with Agent Baker. I didn't have time to make an appointment. I just stopped by to speak to him."

"Just a moment. I'll see if I can locate him." After a call, she looked at me and said, "Mr. Ballard?"

"Yes, Preston Ballard."

"Do you have an I.D.? A driver's license will do."

She barely looked at it, then said, "There's a small lounge on the third floor. You can wait for him there."

What happened next was a shock.

The elevator slowed down at the third floor and stopped. The door opened. I saw Baker walking down the hall away from the elevator with another man. Someone out of breath came out of the stairwell across from the elevator and called out to Baker

"Remember you have reliable contacts in Savannah."

Baker turned to look back and gave a thumbs up, pointing to the man beside him, "He's in touch with both of them, and everything is set. It will happen very soon."

Just as they reached the end of the hallway, the man with Baker turned and smiled, giving a thumbs up sign.

What the fuck?!

It was Evaldo Hauser! For real this time not, a ghost.

My friend in law school, my absent host in Magdalena, who had "needed" me to help his dying father.

I stood there, almost losing my footing as the building tilted. I had to lean against the wall as the elevator door slowly closed with a little ding, ding, and started back down toward the lobby on the first floor.

The same receptionist was at the desk. She looked up and smiled, "What happened? That was a very short meeting."

I just nodded.

"I want to tell Baker that I appreciate all that he has done. I will send him a text."

"Yes, send him a text. Ed is a really nice guy."

I managed to smile back. "That's just what I thought when I first met him."

"Oh, where was that?"

"In Savannah."

She gave me a knowing look.

"Of course, and I will send him a text." I wanted to say thanks for all the lies. It's always a pleasure to be used and humiliated. Watch your back with Evaldo Hauser.

Good Luck and give my best to Queenie and Charley. Savannah was a blast.

Preston Ballard.

I stumbled to my car, took a deep breath, and began beating my fist on the steering wheel yelling "Fuck, fuck, fuck."

I backed out and peeled rubber out of the parking lot, jamming the gas pedal down and trying to focus on what had just happened.

After a few miles, I looked at my speedometer and saw I was doing eighty, weaving in and out of traffic and leaving blaring horns and swerving cars behind me.

"So what? I just gave the finger to the F.B.I."

It was late afternoon. I had skipped breakfast and missed lunch. My hands were trembling. I needed to eat and calm down. A McDonalds loomed in front of me.

The place was almost empty. It was that in between time when lunch was over and the evening rush had not started. I ordered two double Big Macs with cheese, fries, and a chocolate shake, then took a booth in the back.

I started with the shake to get a quick rush, then unpacked the burgers and fries.

I began taking slow, deliberate bites.

Organizing the layout of the food helped me see that I desperately needed to organize my life. My heart stopped pounding and the muscles in my back relaxed.

The A. C. was making a soft, whirring noise and something clicked in my mind.

My hamburger bites made me think of another 'B' word. That was it. Bats.

And I was suddenly back in Magdalena with Padre Liborio, watching the bats lifting out of the rooftops. I thought of King Momo and wondered whose misery he would expose next.

Poor Chavela, betrayed by Chingo over and over. She had known what terrible report would be coming from King Momo as he rode his white horse toward us, so at the next Carnival she would run inside again to avoid being humiliated. What would King Momo say about me then? Something like this?

This Gringo sighs and shakes his head,
So many people want him dead,
He needs a hit of Bolivian cocaine
To make his world seem right again."

"O Bolivia prima rosa,"" was the song that was played over and over again on the loudspeakers around the town square that night. I swore then that I would never return to Magdalena and sit on one of benches in front of the Hauser's house, fronting on the town square.

We had been waiting for the bats to rise that evening, watching the young boys carry wooden platters of pan de arroz fresh out of the big clay ovens behind each home.

I cleared off the McDonald's wrappings and the little packets of ketchup, salt, and pepper from the table. Then let myself come to terms with my shock, anger, and confusion.

I knew that Ed Baker and the rest of the F.B.I. team would be amused by my reaction to seeing Evaldo, my friend at the very center, the "locus classicus" of the drug trade. I saw it as "deception" and I was through with it all—Bolivia, Evaldo, cocaine, C. I.'s.

I no longer would have to live my life as a tool, a low-level worker for the F.B.I. I was probably finished with my job at the law firm, not to mention, finished with the judge, and maybe with my mother.

I was sick of being a stooge. I was leaving Dodge. That decision was a good thing. I would follow Delores to Switzerland and make her understand that not only had I come back, but that I was not going anywhere without her.

Delores, I liked to tell myself, whose childhood had been spent dodging bombs and being rescued, would, I knew, stay with Khumar out of loyalty until he died. I would be patient and wait. Then she could stay with me until I died. That would make me happy.

It was now late afternoon. I listened to the traffic and took another sip of my milk shake, then reached for my cell.

I couldn't put it off any longer, and I tapped my mother's name on the screen. Her phone rang, and then her recorded message came on.

"This is Louise Ballard. I can't come to the phone right now, but…"

This was interrupted as my mother answered.

"Preston, is that you?"

"Hi, Mom. Yes, I just came in last night."

"We've been so worried about you."

I could tell from her overly sweet, slurred speech that she had already started drinking. In the background, I could hear the judge yell "If that's Preston, tell him to be careful."

I heard my mother, "Just be quiet so I can talk."

I could hear her fumbling with something, and then a crash.

She hissed, "You made me drop my glass!"

Then the judge's voice sounded closer. "Give me the phone and clean up the glass." There was a pause and then the judge came on.

"Hello, Preston? Where the hell are you?"

"Where the hell are you?" I shot back. "I'm at the McDonalds, near Delray Beach."

"Well, the F.B.I. is running in circles looking for you."

"I was just there."

"Oh. Well, that's good. I'm glad to hear it."

"Are you at home?"

"Home! Preston, are you crazy?"

"I'm going that way."

"Dammit, Preston, didn't the F.B.I. tell you anything?"

"Like what?"

"It's that friend of yours, that Ivondo, or something like that."

"Evaldo. Evaldo Hauser."

"Right. Anyway, he showed up a week or two ago, saying that the cocaine shipment is on the way from Bolivia. It's on a large fishing trawler. It was headed for Tybee."

There was a long pause. I could hear the judge take a heavy breath. "That's the island near Savannah."

"Yes."

"That's all been changed. Savannah is filled with drug dealers and under-cover police, not to mention the F.B.I."

"So what island are we talking about?"

The judge evidently turned to my mother and whispered something that sounded like, "Jesus, Louise, he doesn't know anything."

There was a pause and then my mother came on the line.

"Preston, Preston, just be careful and keep quiet. Don't ruin the plan and get yourself hurt."

"Ruin what?"

"We're going to be set, Preston. Just keep quiet and it will all work out."

Then the judge was back on the line.

"Just stay away from the Blue Palm for the next week or so. Things will calm down after the drugs come in and are distributed. Dammit, Preston, pay attention. The drugs are coming into the Blue Palm on a fishing trawler in the next day or so. You were just in Bolivia. Didn't you understand what your friends were doing for us? For your mother and for you?"

The light finally turned on in my head. "So that's why the hotel is closed for the week?"

"Exactly. All the guests are gone, along with most of the employees, except for a small kitchen staff for Lefcourt and his wife."

"And Khumar is leaving for Switzerland?"

"No, that's just a cover story. Khumar and his wife will be sealed off on the top floor of the hotel until all the excitement dies down. Lefcourt and his new wife will be up there taking care of them in case there's any trouble."

"What kind of trouble is that?"

"Well, the usual kind. The Mexican cartel. But now your friend Guzman and his Cuban ragtags might show up. But don't worry. The F.B.I. has it all scoped out."

I let all the lies and deceptions sink in.

"As I understand it, you and my mother are into this business in a big way."

"Absolutely not!" the judge yelled, trying to sound indignant.

"Khumar and Lefcourt put it all together with the Bolivians. Your mother and I are not involved in this deal in any way. I've always had business dealings with Khumar.

That was never a secret. All we know is what people tell us, and we pass that along to the F.B.I."

"So, either way, you come out winners."

"That's not fair, Preston."

I had heard enough. "So, are you and my mother at home now?"

"Of course not. We're in a safe place until this business is over and things calm down."

"And where is this 'safe place?'"

The judge gave a little chuckle. "You'll never guess?"

"I give up."

"We're at Satterwhites."

"That dump?!"

"That was years ago, Preston. You are behind the times. It's all luxury lakefront condos now, with a two-star restaurant."

"That sounds just perfect. Save me a place at that underwater table." I hung up before the judge could answer.

12.

So my mother and the judge were sheltering in place at Satterwhites. I needed to think about where the money to develop the place and to build the new condos was coming from.

Earlier, at the hotel, Lefcourt had said that Delores and Simon Khumar were leaving for Switzerland. But the judge contradicted that and said that they were staying at the hotel, sealed off on the top floor with the Lefcourts taking care of them.

Ann was a nurse, so that made sense.

Delores? So Switzerland would be her first choice. I wondered how Delores could get out of the country with all of the Bolivian connections that she must have had in place to send message delivered by King Momo. Was it too late for Delores to get out? Now, would she leave her bedridden husband?

I felt the way I always felt: Outside, locked out. Things happened to me as a child that left me with no place to go except to stay outside. I was the ultimate outsider who belonged nowhere and couldn't read the exit signs.

My role was the outsider, the extra hired at the last minute. Just as in Bolivia, I was the one who had not had a horse sent for me, the Gringo. I could not ride back to Magdalena with the others, so I had to go upriver alone. I would always be served the roasted Blue Jays.

I mustn't complain if I wanted to survive.

But now, I wanted to be an insider. Delores was an insider—to what extent I wasn't sure—and the caregiver of her dying husband.

I could be inside with her and help. All I could offer her as an outsider was a list of things I was not. I wasn't inside the law, I was the person who didn't belong, and ended up being ordered to go to Bolivia for no reason except to satisfy a request to my firm from the F.B.I. and because I had a friend from Bolivia. Not a real friend, not the friend I thought I had in law school. This kind of reasoning never had an end and reminded me of the conversations I heard growing up.

The judge almost never ate at our house, but on rare occasions, he would arrive for dinner unannounced as if to say, 'I'm here because I couldn't think of any other place to be.'

My mother would be wearing her blue dress and would have a drink already mixed and waiting. She would sit on the arm of his chair as the judge sank down beside her. She would stroke his arm and ask, "Was it a bad day for you?"

The judge would say something like, "It was godawful, that's what it was.

Listening to case after case of drunks, perverts, and liars of every stripe and color.

Humanity in the raw."

My mother would make sympathetic sounds and then brighten up and say "You know what? Let's just go out for a nice dinner and forget all about it."

What followed was predictable, continuing sometimes for almost an hour, with breaks for another drink before they left.

As I grew older, my mother and I would make bets and laugh at what we would call the "Naming of the names." The first move in the game would be my mother suggesting a possible restaurant for the evening, like the Fox Head Inn. The game had no point but did pass the time before they went out. Sometimes I went with them.

Sometimes I did not.

It had been a long day.

I left the McDonald's and headed for my mother's home on the beach that the judge had bought for her. I found the key under the mat at the front door.

I had not been there for a long time. I had lived there for summer vacations from college and law school, but my mother was always there. Now, I walked through the empty rooms, surprised at how small the house seemed. I remembered every room exactly. Nothing had changed, but now everything seemed to have changed.

As always, I felt like an outsider. It was as if there were two houses: the house I wished I could belong in and the one that I never would.

Without thinking about it, I knew I could never spend the night here again.

Coming in, I had walked through the house and turned on the lights in the hallway and then turned on the lights as I entered each room. Now, as I started to leave I began turning off the lights until for some reason I paused. I was standing in the hallway outside my mother's room and realized I had not even opened her door and looked inside.

Growing up, I had somehow learned that I should not go into her room. My mother never actually said this directly, and probably as a very young child I had been in her room, but now, I could not remember going into her room.

I opened the door, then turned on the lights. At first, everything seemed normal.

Nothing seemed out of place.

There was a small desk in the corner, with a leather box on top with a clasp lock.

I flipped the lid up. Inside, there was a photograph of a man wearing an army uniform with master sergeant's stripes on his sleeves. He was smiling. It was my Uncle Virgil.

There was a letter with the photograph. I knew some of his history.

Uncle Virgil had enlisted in a munitions regiment a few months before the War began. After Pearl Harbor, his regiment was activated and by the end of 1942 his outfit was in England training for the invasion. Shortly after D Day his unit was shipped to France and began ferrying munitions forward to the combat troops on the front lines.

After the Allied invasion of France, his outfit was close enough to the port of Cherbourg to move ammunition supplies by truck up to the front lines. But as the Allies pushed the Germans back, the distance from the port to the front lines grew longer and longer, until large convoys of trucks had to be supplemented by trains hauling boxcars loaded with high explosives.

Uncle Virgil was assigned with another man in his unit, an old friend named Richard "Richie" Green, to accompany one of those munition trains loaded with the explosives from the harbor of Cherbourg to the front lines.

The danger lay in marauding German ME109 fighter planes. There were two French engineers running the locomotive. My Uncle Virgil and his buddy Richie, were on the platform at the rear of the caboose, taking a smoke.

The trains would leave Cherbourg after dark, so most of the trip was at night to avoid the German planes. But at dawn there would be about four hours of daylight when Uncle Virgil and Richie would sit on platform at the back waving to farmers and pretty girls as the train rolled past.

Then, without warning, two German fighters dove out of the sun, strafing the train before disappearing behind some clouds. Without thinking, my Uncle Virgil and Richie climbed over the back rail of the caboose, and were getting ready to jump, certain that explosions were coming, but nothing happened.

The train slowed down to half speed and they saw a man running through the wheat field. He turned and waved at Uncle Virgil and Richie who recognized the French engineer. He had evidently slowed the train down just before jumping off, leaving the locomotive with no one in control.

Uncle Virgil knew that the train had to be stopped, since even a small accident could set off the explosives and that they had been amazingly lucky by dodging the German fighters.

Fortunately, there was a ladder attached to the outside of the caboose that ran from the platform at the rear to the top of the caboose, so they climbed up and then hopped the freight cars back to the locomotive.

They were both good mechanics, and soon figured out how to slow the train down.

There was plenty of coal and they hoped that there was enough water in the boiler to make steam. But they remained unsure how to brake the train if they needed to make a sudden stop, which meant that they would have to continue at the same slow speed they were making now, and use throttle if needed.

I had never heard Uncle Virgil's war story before. At the bottom of the page he had added a brief P. S.

> Here is the number for the bank account I have set up in Preston's name... As far as I can tell, we are the last two in our family, and I wanted him to have it. Maybe it will help him. I have set aside ten thousand dollars for him to use when he needs it. He was my favorite.. I always admired the way he ate that terrible Blue Jay dish you made him eat. I wanted those Blue Jays shot and he did it. I will never understand why you did what you did.
>
> Love anyway, Virgil.

I folded the letter and placed it back on the desk with Uncle Virgil's picture on top, as my mother had left it. I hoped I would be to able sleep undisturbed by the ghosts from my childhood.

I was wrong.

My sleep was uneasy, for in my dreams a parade of images followed each other during the night. Over and over people kept waving to me as they receded into the darkness.

The first images were the most recent; my mother and Judge Talley appeared, warning me to be careful before opening the door then disappearing, with my mother waving goodbye, leaving behind a wailing cry that grew fainter and fainter.

They were replaced by a scene in the town square in Magdalena, where I sat waiting with Chavela as King Momo approached and delivered Delores's cruel message.

Chavela waved to me, and then threw her arms up as if to surrender to the skeletal figure who claimed to know the truths we were trying to hide.

Over and over, other unrecognizable figures would appear, waving to me before melting away like candle wax.

I would never ask my mother about Uncle Virgil's gift. and I hoped I could be like him and drive my life as he had driven that locomotive with no explosions. She had never told me about the money he left me. Another one of her inexplicable acts.

13.

My first job at the law firm had involved the murder of a popular teacher at a local community college. I was assigned to gather a list of witnesses, for a highly publicized murder case at North Florida Community College.

I had felt the judge's hand in this prize assignment. It rankled, but I knew it would be very helpful to my future as a lawyer.

Of course, Judge Talley had recommended me to the firm of Benson & Jones.

Dave Benson, the senior partner, had explained what was needed: a list of people at the College who would throw light on the case. The college was set in the orange groves of Lake County in north Florida, as unlikely a setting for a bloody murder as is possible.

I knew a few of the people at the college from growing up in the next county, but I was glad to see that none of them had made the interview list.

I had started with Community College's President Martin, and found his office in the Hewett Building, named after the local congressman who had secured a grant from the Department of Education in Washington to create a program in Criminal Justice.

My first hint that something could go wrong had been when I had entered the President's outer office. Two secretaries—their nametags said Gladys and Mabel—had been talking to a man I guessed was a dean. Their voices had raised as this Dean was told that a lawyer was there to interview President Martin about "what had happened," and that the list of witnesses was needed right away.

I had found out later that the "lawyer" they were referring to was me.

The dean had cursed under his breath and retreated.

As they watched him go, the secretaries stuck out their tongues and looked at each other with vicious smiles. Then had said together, "The husband did it."

There had been a pause before Gladys stood up and went into the President's office. Then Mabel had turned to me with a sweet as syrup smile.

"Can I help you?"

President Jerome Martin was an ex-Marine who stood up and shook my hand. Of course, he knew Judge Talley and had met my mother at various functions.

I sat down in front of his desk and waited.

He was nervous and after a moment of arranging his papers, he coughed.

"So, how much do you know?"

"Not much. Just that your P.E. director has been accused of murdering his wife, one of your teachers. And that the Community College has hired my firm, Benson & Jones. I have been asked to put together a preliminary list of witnesses."

President Martin nodded and went into what was probably his prepared remarks about the murder.

"I want to say, first of all, that everyone at North Florida Community College is shocked at the brutal murder of one our teachers. She was loved and admired by our students and faculty.

"I have instructed everyone to cooperate fully with the investigation."

I countered with my own canned statement, saying how I appreciated the President's willingness to cooperate, and how I wanted to emphasize that I was at the college only for a preliminary identification of people he thought could throw light on what had happened.

I had expected the typical public relations statements about the murder, justice being served and the rights of the accused, the presumption of innocence until proven guilty. Instead, I sensed that the man accused had already been condemned.

The victim, Ann Marie Castenaro, had been beloved by the President, as well as all of the other faculty and staff I would go on to interview.

Everyone at the college had warned her that Roger Norton, the P. E. Director, was borderline psychotic. It turned out, they were right.

This had been his third marriage.

When Ann Marie announced her engagement, President Martin had called her into his office. He had begged her to break her engagement and leave town, assuring her that he knew of faculty positions in the system that he could secure for her.

But Ann Marie claimed that Norton had changed. That she loved him, and that she was devoted to his two children from previous marriages.

And so they married.

For about a year, all seemed to be going well.

Then one night, before they went to bed, they were watching a favorite TV show the kids liked, and Norton went to pick up a pizza.

When he had returned home, he found his wife dead. Her throat had been cut.

The children had been covered in blood and had been hiding in their bedroom.

Norton swore he was innocent, but no one believed him even though witnesses at the pizza restaurant remembered seeing him there at the time of the murder. There were no security cameras and the receipt had been lost.

At almost the same time, there was a break-in at a house across town, but the intruder had run away when the owners came home. No one would connect these two crimes until much later.

I handed the President what my law firm called a briefing paper, with dates for interviews.

After about thirty minutes, the Dean gave me a list of ten people at the college that my firm should consider as primary witnesses. Then another list of witnesses who could substantiate certain key facts about both Norton and his murdered wife, their character and background, family, church and community involvement.

A time frame leading up to and after the murder was established. The police were already heavily involved and rumor had it that in the next few days they were going to arrest Norton for murdering his wife.

It was clear that Benson & Jones had been hired to protect the college's reputation, and because the college was a state school, the state needed to be protected from future lawsuits.

As I started to leave President Martin's office, a man dressed in mechanic's coveralls knocked on the door. President Martin had let him in and had introduced him as Gunny McBride, which, I would learn later, was Marine talk for Gunnery Sergeant Jason McBride.

"Gunny runs our motor pool and takes care of everything mechanical at the college," President Martin explained. We both retired from the Corps at the same time, and I talked him into coming to North Florida with me."

Gunny had piercing blue eyes and blond hair that was turning gray. We shook hands. "Pleased to meet you," Gunny said. Then turned to the President, "Is this the man from the law firm."

President Martin nodded.

Gunny gave me an ice-cold stare.

"I hope Norton fries." He said.

My involvement had started the morning after my dinner at the Blue Palm with the Lefcourts. Amaya Wheeler, my supervisor at Benson & Jones, had called to say I needed to finish up the report on the North Florida Community College murder investigation before I went flying off to Bolivia.

"I thought that there would be a trial. And that they had found out who had killed the young English professor," I blurted out. "Ann Marie something."

"Things have changed. The F.B.I. is involved and it seems there are connections to other things you might know about."

"Connections to what?"

I wouldn't know the answer to my question until later. Even then it was only suspicions with no facts to support them, but I had been right.

Ann Marie had been killed because she knew too much about her husband and Gunny's secret drug deals. The intruder who was arrested for the murder because he had her ring, was just a drunkard who had slipped the ring off her bloody finger when he broke into her home. He fled when he heard the girls screaming because they saw him as he left.

Later, they identified him in a line-up and the case had been closed.

I never felt the real killer had been arrested.

Later when I returned from Bolivia my life had been turned upside down. I hardly ever thought about that North Florida Community College murder.

But Amaya Wheeler would only say, in her usual deadening flat tone that gave nothing away, "Ed Baker will pick you up at 8:00 in the morning."

I knew I was trapped again. I wasn't sure what piece of evidence had been uncovered, but I somehow understood that I was in the world of "unknown knowns".

That something had brought together Bolivian cocaine and the murdered English teacher.

It was only later that I learned that it was Gunny McBride who connected them both.

The next morning Ed Baker picked me up. I mumbled a greeting, and he gave me a slight nod. We drove along the old coastal highway, heading north.

Ed opened with "I hear you're a rich man, a hotel owner."

"How did you know that?"

"Word gets around."

"Am I being investigated?"

"Not that I know of. "My boss at Benson & Jones said something about connections between drugs and North Florida Community College, and some of the people I might have interviewed when I was there. Do you know anything about that?"

Ed frowned, and said "Do you remember a man called Gunny McBride?"

I took a deep breath. I recognized the name but couldn't remember much more.

"I think we met briefly. He came into the Community College President's office just as I was leaving. He had something to do with mechanical stuff, but I'm not really sure what he did."

He oversaw the college motor pool, several trucks, and faculty cars, as well as handled the maintenance on things like that. Making sure the tanks were full and that all the vehicles passed safety inspections."

"As I said, we met briefly. Not much more than shaking hands saying good to meet you.

"Nothing else?"

"No, nothing else."

We drove in silence for a few miles as I waited for the other shoe to drop. Finally, Ed got tired of waiting for me to say something more.

"One of our team found a connection between the Suárez people and someone at the Community College," Ed finally admitted.

"I missed that."

"One of them was Gunny McBride."

"Holy shit!" I said aloud. I couldn't help myself.

"He was tight with the president at the college." I stopped, trying to remember. "I forget his name."

"Martin," Ed prompted. "President Martin and Gunny were old Marine buddies."

"Were they just buddies or partners?"

"We think they were partners, but the President wasn't involved in drugs. At least, we don't think so.

"Martin, you might say, was a partner without knowing it. At least that's what we believe now. Gunny was using the friendship with Martin to hide his drug operations.

"One of the President's secretaries had been at the college forever and knew everything that went on. She would feed Gunny all kinds of information—some useful, some not so useful, and hide things from the President and other faculty members.

"Gunny used the College motor pool vehicles to move illegal drugs to safe places. The secretary submitted phony records about vehicle usage and repairs. Martin never questioned them about anything, and evidently just signed whatever was put in front of him."

"So why am I on this trip? I just met them briefly to develop a list of witnesses for the murder trial that was dropped."

"Which one was that?"

"You don't remember?"

"I've got a lot on my plate," Baker said.

"Let me remind you," I said.

"I had returned to Benson & Jones with the two lists of witnesses. I included a brief paragraph warning that President Martin and others at NFCC had already decided that Norton was guilty of murdering his wife and I, myself, thought he was guilty of murder.

"But, as it turned out, the case against Roger Norton never came to trial. The state was never able to prove that Norton was not at the pizza hut at the time of the murder, and a neighbor remembered seeing Norton get out of his car holding a large square box similar to those sold to carry pizzas.

"No other evidence turned up. After a couple of years, the active investigation of the murder of Ann Marie Mason stopped. The case remains unsolved.

"Norton left his two daughters with his parents and took a job in Montana. Then he dropped out of sight.

That was the end of the case. I heard that President Martin had retired and moved away.

"I was sure that most of the people at the college were distressed that the case remained open but unsolved.

Gradually things returned to normal. I heard they appointed a new president for NFCC.

Then, two years later, there was an accident outside of town. A man named Kingston was driving drunk and ran off the road into a ditch.

The policeman, who stopped to help him, did a routine check and found that Kingston had a record and there were warrants out for his arrest.

"A gold ring was found in his possession, a ring he claimed he bought at a pawn shop. It had the inscription 'AM + R' and someone remembered that Roger Norton had asked if his wife's wedding ring had been found.

The case was reopened.

Kingston had just finished a two-year prison term for theft. His old cellmate testified that Kingston had bragged about killing a woman. In addition, one of Norton's daughters, who was seven at the time of the murder, identified him as a man who had come to their home a week before the murder to do some minor home repairs. Kingston took a guilty plea to avoid a death sentence.

I had been relieved when I had completed the final list of witnesses for the murder case at North Florida Community College. Amaya Wheeler had actually smiled at me, and though she did not bring herself to say good work, the atmosphere in her office lifted.

She had told me to wait for my next assignment and then asked if I kept up with my friend from Bolivia.

I guessed that the judge must have mentioned my law school friend, Evaldo Hauser.

At that point, there was, in fact, no drug bust at the Blue Palm Hotel as I had I suspected. There were rumors about the drug shipment on the ocean-going fishing trawler but had been diverted. It had either found another port or turned back and docked where it had started at Cartagena.

No one was sure what had happened. Either someone was tipped off by an informant, or the trawler had turned back because of a hurricane that was brewing. No one was arrested, and I had not heard from Evaldo. I thought that his silence could mean that he wanted to protect me in some way. What I did not know was a good thing.

Guzman told me that the Khumar had left for a clinic, maybe one in Switzerland, but I would find no trace of Delores and Simon after many deep searches on the internet. They had vanished.

I assumed that Sandy Lefcourt was still the manager at the Blue Palm, and that he must know where the Khumars were, but he had been vague about their whereabouts. I guessed that Delores and the doctors had kept Khumar alive somehow.

I still occasionally saw Guzman at the Cuba Libre bar. He always slapped me on the shoulder and smiled. We talked about the political situation in Cuba.

Then, on a visit, he gave me a quizzical look and asked if I knew about a big real estate development for rich people called Satterwhites. This, in itself was not unusual.

The place had assumed, even for north Florida, a reputation as a hideaway for the extremely wealthy. Satterwhites was seen as a safe retreat from the C.O.V.I.D.-19 virus.

What worried me more than the new virus was that Guzman seemed to have connected Satterwhites with me.

"Why do you ask about Satterwhites?"

"Someone named Aster called and said she has a cake for you."

I could have asked several questions, such as how did Sally's daughter know how to get in touch with me? Or why should I care about Satterwhites? Or what the cake meant? Instead, it was Guzman who stated the obvious.

"Satterwhites is a long drive just to give you a cake."

I turned and looked at him, hoping that Aster was relaying a message from Delores who must have said not to use her name. So Aster had used the word "cake" trusting that I would understand. It meant that the Khumars were at Satterwhites. They must have been warned that a drug raid was coming to the Blue Palm and had set up the rumor that they were in Europe to cover their tracks.

"When did Aster call?"

"About an hour ago."

"Can you text me her number?"

I turned to go, but Guzman wouldn't give up.

"You should stop. Don't even think of going there.'"

"How is that?"

"You're deceiving yourself. You think you can go on like this, as if you have all of eternity in front of you to keep on making deadly mistakes.

"The ship is still coming from Cartagena; it will bring a hurricane of violence—You must be on your guard. Get out of its way and hope to God that your secret love can do the same."

I knew that he was right, but what could I do?

I knew that Delores must have asked Aster to call me about her mother's "cake" and I knew that Delores didn't care about her own danger, only about her husband's safety. She had asked Aster to call about the cake because, my heart told me, she cared about my safety.

I can't give her up, was my constant thought.

But what about Guzman and his warning.? A cake? How absurd. And yet it was Guzman who had said, "She wants to see you."

Maybe I had made that up, heard what I wanted to hear. I was the outsider, outside the real story.

15.

I left Guzman still not knowing what to do, what to feel. Did Delores love me?

There were signs everywhere, but signs were not truths.

I was not reliable. With signs I could prove anything.

A cake? Common sense provided only contradictory evidence. I knew how I felt about Delores, but what did she feel about me. What was I worth?

Messages were stacking up on my phone. Messages from the F.B.I. to call immediately or face serious consequences, messages from Benson & Jones asking for my latest assessment about the case at NFCC. There was a message from Ann Glaser saying she knew that Lefcourt had talked to me and that I should call her. A message from Judge Talley asking why in hell I didn't answer the phone once in a while?

I decided that Ann would have the best advice about how to get in touch with Delores, so I returned her call, with a mental note that she was now Ann Lefcourt.

Ann answered, "Preston, I heard you were back from…was it somewhere in South America?"

"Bolivia."

"Right. I wasn't sure. I had to look it up. What was in Bolivia?"

"My law firm sent me. It's a long story."

"I hope you will get a bonus for going."

"I doubt it. Things don't work that way."

"Sometimes they do. Were there snakes?"

"Yes, lots. As well as bats, monkeys, tarantulas, and capybaras."

"What's that last one?"

"It's the world's biggest rat," I answered.

There was a long pause.

"You heard I'm married?"

"I saw Sandy at the hotel. Congratulations. He said there are big changes at the hotel. Renovations and so forth."

"Yes. It's a crazy time, even with the hotel shut down."

I needed to know more, so I took a chance and asked. "I hear Khumar and his wife are at a place called Satterwhites."

"Yes, that's right. Did Sandy tell you that?"

I hesitated. "Just in passing. I thought they were on their way to Europe?"

"Yes. Switzerland. Mr. Khumar is very ill."

"Are they leaving soon?"

"It's complicated. Delores is trying to make the arrangements now." Ann hesitated, and then continued.

"Mr. Khumar's condition. He is getting rapidly worse. I try not to ask too many questions."

I took this as Ann's way of saying she didn't want to continue talking about what was happening with the Khumars or the hotel.

After a few goodbyes and a stay-in-touch, I hung up.

I felt that my life was now focused on interpreting signs placed before me. The cake, Khumar's health, what Delores really wanted, if the F.B.I. could be trusted, if I still had a job at Benson & Jones, if my mother really cared about what happened to me, if the bank account set up by Uncle Virgil was still in my name.

All of these situations seem so bizarre, so ambiguous. Was it normal for a law firm to hand over a new hire—me—to the F.B.I. for a criminal investigation? Was it normal for the woman I loved to tell me not to come back? Was it normal for my mother to try to force me to eat roasted Blue Jays?

After talking to Ann, I decided that I would drive up to Satterwhites.

I knew how much I loved Delores, but somehow it was no longer possible for me to prove it to her. This inability was the worst thing of all.

Signs of love are not proof, since signs are ambiguous and anyone can produce false signs or words. But, paradoxically, this ambiguous quality of language was all I had.

As I drove, I became more and more committed to stop questioning myself about what to believe, and to simply declare my love for Delores again. To demand that she say what it was that she needed me to do. Beyond this, I wasn't sure. Whatever she would say in reply would be her answer. I would live with it. Or die.

Soon the highway broadened out into four lanes, with a well-kept grass divider in the middle. Up ahead, I could see an entrance with a large gate and a small guard house. There was a sign that said Satterwhites: Members and Guests Only. Beyond the guard house the road disappeared into the trees. I wasn't sure what to expect.

The guard came out with a friendly smile and said, "How can I help you?"

All I could think of was to say that I was there to see Mrs. Khumar.

"Are you Mr. Ballard?"

"Yes. Preston Ballard."

He asked for some I.D. and I handed him my driver's license. He disappeared into the guard house, and after a moment came back and handed me my license and a white envelope with my name on it.

He pointed to a small parking lot and said, "You can turn around over there."

I was stunned. So this was it, I thought. She doesn't even want to see me.

I parked and opened the letter. My heart soared. It wasn't a goodbye:

Dear Preston,

Ann Lefcourt called and said you might come.

I need to tell you this: We have a private jet. There is a separate platform for private flights. We will board Simon with his doctor and nurse at 4:30. I will be at the loading gate until then. We will depart from Jacksonville International at 5:00 pm, then on to Dulles for Simon's final examination. If that goes well, then to Paris. After another exam by the doctors there, a final drive to Switzerland. It's nicer than the freight elevator to the sub-basement.

Delores

I sat in the car, clutching her letter. I thought about how once, at the Far Cottage, I had asked her about Khumar. She had said that she couldn't imagine her life without him. She stopped, and then added, as if explaining, "He will need me. When he dies, I will be with him."

"Don't say that!"

"I couldn't let him go alone."

"But I can't go there."

"No, you have to stay behind."

I started the car and turned toward Jacksonville.

I would follow her to the ends of the ends of the earth, and beyond.

Then I wondered, Did she mean that she would be with her husband when he died or that she would die with him?

How was I supposed to interpret her words? I had no idea, but I would go to the airport.

16.

I should have known that I would face an attack of cluster headaches, what I called "my cluster fucks" when I returned from Bolivia and needed a place to crash so they could run their course. Delores' note bringing relief and misery mixed together set the attack off.

I rented a rundown mobile home at Sunny Dale Park twelve miles from the Blue Palm.

I wasn't sure if I still had a job at the law firm of Benson & Jones, but a splitting headache prevented me from writing a coherent sentence on my report of what I had seen in Bolivia for the F.B.I.'s Task Force.

Ed Baker had sent a message saying my report was urgently needed. But I needed a report on my own life—what Delores meant, what my friendship with the Hausers meant, where the drug money would end up.

I remembered that when I was eighteen in Clover, I was arrested for what seemed to the sheriff for driving under the influence. He was shocked when I passed the breathalyzer test. It was the fact that the judge lived with my mother and me, controlling our lives with our consent and desperation for money.

I tried to tell the sheriff what the neurologist had said about the headaches that would come like lightning strikes, splitting my head open and fogging my brain and my vision. The pain was so intense that I would dissociate from my experiences to the point of not knowing where I was or what I was doing. The doctor said such headaches came from hell. Those were his words.

The neurologist gave me Imitrex to inject into my thigh when the flashing aura, which signaled an attack, came on.

The doctor explained that the pain from cluster headaches was worse than the pain from migraines and was known to have driven people to suicide. It is the worst pain that is self-generated and comes only after a person has survived a crisis, never during the ordeal A new kind of hell, he said.

Having survived the rivers filled with crocodiles and piranhas, bullets from Chingo in San Ramón, vampire bats in Magdalena, King Momo's warning, and the cruel command by the woman I loved not to come back to her, the cluster headaches hit at full strength.

I had learned to fear the headaches even more than the overturned oxcart or eating the roasted giant rat or Chingo's drunken violence or Delores's final words came closest to the pain of the cluster headaches.

I always felt that my life was series of events that I was helpless to control or understand. The diagnosis of the cluster headaches explained, at least, how I processed stress. They were a punishment from my unconscious self for being inadequate.

Whether I was transporting supplies up a Bolivian river or watching a hungry leopard debate if I was worth the trouble, I simply had to accept the pain and know that it was inevitable.

Dissociation, the doctor had continued, separated me temporarily from the danger. But when the danger had passed, I my head would split. I would feel shattered by the emotional impact that expressed in physical pain.

I needed a place like Sunnyside Mobile Home Park where the crash could happen.

As I dealt with my headaches, I was free to think about the role that Evaldo played in the labyrinth of drug trafficking and competition with the rival Mexicans, the Suárez family.

Evaldo, the ever-changing. Evaldo, the phantom. Was he a good friend who expected me to trust him, not question him?

He had invited me to visit his family in Magdalena--an invitation that suggested to my supervisor, Amaya, that I could be of use to the firm's arrangement with the F.B.I.

She had urged me, ordered me in so many words and assured me. I should accept my friend's invitation and also the F.B.I.'s assignment.

I was told not to worry: it was a win-win situation. I felt unable to say no. So, I had accepted Evaldo's invitation and Amaya's Wheeler's assignment to observe and report on the coca production and shipment. She said I had done a good job with the murder case at the community college and this assignment was the same, except in Bolivia and about drugs.

The cluster headaches came from a repression so strong that it felt as if my brain split into two in the most dramatic physical way.

Doctor Suter had told me that cluster headaches almost always came at night just after falling asleep. They would continue every night for two or three weeks and then disappear for five or six months. For some reason, I was always surprised when they came.

When I came back from the Beni, I had enough memories to trigger cluster headaches for a lifetime.

At night I would dream of King Momo's skeletal form, and his words that seemed to penetrate all my carefully built-up defenses; dreams of the glittering eyes of the cattle heads lined up by the runway in San Ramón, or the bullet from Chingo's revolver blowing away a bottle of beer.

And here I was back home in Florida, sure I had lost Delores forever, to then find Uncle Virgil's letter and realizing that my mother had never told me that there was money for me from him.

I was also facing pressures from the F.B.I. and my law firm.

How could I summarize what I had seen in the Beni?

Profits from the drugs were astronomical only if the drugs could reach their destination. I read in the local papers that a thirty-million-dollar haul was seized from just one cargo ship in Savannah.

With my headaches, I did what I always did. I used that split in my mind to push all of those thoughts down deeper and deeper.

In my mobile home at Sunnyside, I could keep in touch with Ann Lefcourt at the Blue Palm in order to find out what had happened to Delores.

I waited a week and then started sending emails to her old address. They were never answered. Then I started getting responses from Google saying that this address was no longer active. Then I got a call from Ann Lefcourt saying that Delores had sent a request to get in touch with me on her behalf. Delores wanted me to stop trying to reach her and that she would contact me as soon as Simon's condition had stabilized.

My first thought was to leave immediately for Switzerland, but Ann persuaded me to trust Delores and wait for developments.

Ann had agreed to be our go-between and suggested that I finish my report on the Bolivian cocaine and write the "I quit" letter to Amaya Wheeler, the one swore to myself that I would submit.

I called Benson & Jones saying I needed two or three more weeks to finish my report.

My mother and Judge Talley called to say they were hiding at Satterwhites because the Corona Virus was spreading so rapidly. I didn't ask about Uncle Virgil's letter or the money left for me.

I stayed at Sunnyside and fell into a routine of working on my reports for Ed Baker and Benson & Jones in the morning and then taking a break for lunch.

The internet was full of conspiratorial reports that cocaine could prevent or cure the virus, a false hope which would lead to more profits for the cartels. I was sure the cartels would welcome the news that promised increased sales.

The explosive spread of the virus ravaged the unprotected coca planters, and the cocaine market would soon collapse. But for the moment, the promise of new, safer routes to get the coca to the markets in the States created a boom in the economy of the coca trade.

I continued writing my reports in my trailer. My goal had been a page a day, but as I struggled with my headaches, a page became half a page and then a paragraph.

The Imitrex injections left me in a zombie stupor.

I would start the same sentence over and over and leave out important details of time and place.

I covered my eyes with an old newspaper, leaned back and let the morning sun warm the dull ache still in my head.

One day, as I went through my 'newspaper over my head' routine, a passing car slowed down outside, then it stopped.

I could hear the engine idling. I waited, but the car didn't move.

Without opening my eyes, I waved my arm and yelled, "It's. O.K. I'm just resting."

There was wild laughter from the car and a woman's voice, "He's just resting!" followed by more laughter, and the car's horn blowing.

I sat up, and looked over the porch where I was sitting. I could see Queenie and Charley in the back seat waving at me. Ed Baker was behind the wheel.

He waved and said, "Get in. I'll buy you breakfast."

I tried to stand up but couldn't make it and fell back into my chair. All I could manage was "Oh, shit!"

Charley got out of the car, came over, and pulled me up.

"You forget. Queenie is a trained masseuse."

He pushed me into the back seat. Charley got in the front seat beside Ed, and we pulled away.

"Wow!" Queenie said. "This is a neat place. Some of these trailers are really old."

"I know some people," I said. "I can get you one cheap."

Queenie smiled. "We could be neighbors."

We had breakfast at a restaurant called Flapjacks. Or rather, they had breakfast.

I knew that my cluster headaches wouldn't permit more than coffee.

I listened as Ed Baker filled me in on the latest developments from the world of cocaine smuggling. Savannah was now a major port of entry for bringing in cocaine.

The old cartel routes through Mexico were being bypassed. I had been sent to Bolivia to report on exactly this major change from land to sea, its effects on the Mexican cartels and the Bolivian rival families such as the Hausers.

It was becoming impossible to report on what I did not understand: the drug shipment from the Beni to Brazil, a shipment helped by the Mexican cartel members, the Suarezes, but then cut loose from them to turn the money over to the Hausers. This dangerous plan from the Beni to Brazil to the States was deadly.

It was shocking to me that old cargo ships that could carry tons of product were on the market, starting at eighteen million, and there were plans to buy one of these ships in order to increase the payoff.

Queenie and Charley understood what was happening in this new world far better than I did, but I was the one who had to write the two reports.

"Isn't a cargo ship easy to spot?" I asked.

"Not always."

"They must cost a lot of money," I said, trying to understand what this had to do with smuggling cocaine successfully whether for the criminal Suarezes or the idealist Hausers who were also criminal.

"The current price is about nineteen million, and your old friend Evaldo Hauser just bought one."

I stirred my coffee, trying to sort this out, then shook my head.

"He doesn't have that kind of money."

"We're not asking him to pay for it."

Queenie jumped in and said "He's on our side now Completely. Hook, line and sinker.."

I looked at Ed.

"I saw him at your office."

Ed shrugged.

"We thought that might have happened. You should have come up and said hello."

Ed's casual view of my encounters with the all of this, including the Suárez brothers, was beginning to piss me off.

"I was always terrified in Bolivia. Arturo Suárez doesn't fool around. He was sure I was there to steal his family's money or put him jail…or both. It would have been a big help if you could have let me know more about what was happening."

"You did a great job," Queenie said. "Ed has always said so."

Charley chimed in. "You should hear Evaldo's account of seeing you watching him near Tybee Island. He couldn't believe it."

I gave up. I pulled out my Imitrex syringe. "This is what the Beni did to me."

Ed gave a guilty smile.

"Don't worry, we are definitely not asking you to go back."

"That's just F.B.I. speak for, 'But we are going to ask you to go somewhere else.'"

I mused aloud.

"Yes, but it's a place you know."

Queenie patted my arm.

"We'll be a team again. Isn't it thrilling?"

I groaned.

"Jesus, you don't mean Savannah."

"Our public is waiting."

I couldn't help but add, "Yes, and all their guns are loaded."

****

I finally turned in my reports to the F.B.I. and to Amaya Wheeler, but events were moving too fast. By the time I had it on Ed Baker's desk it was outdated.

For the moment, the Beni was flush with drug money. Landlocked, and isolated by mountains and jungle, Bolivia sat squarely in the center of South America, with its rivers and hundreds of miles of flat grasslands and mountains. It's ideal, not just for growing coca or for processing it, but its isolation makes it possible for small airfields to spring up along its borders.

Savannah, located at confluence of the Savannah River and the Atlantic Ocean had become the port of choice for the drug cartels.

"We reserved a motel room in your name," Ed Baker smiled. "In Savannah, not in Bolivia."

For a few hectic months, Savannah was overwhelmed with large cargo ships carrying cocaine. It was routine for agents to find bags of cocaine stuffed in garbage bins. The crew of one ship had covered a huge shipment of cocaine with piles of junk metal.

No one could foresee that the drug market would crash as Covid-19 began circulating through the unprotected rural populations of the coca producing farms.

For now, Savannah had become a 'gold rush' city, and like Sherman's march to the sea in 1864, the virus grew closer and closer.

I left for Savannah thinking I would do this one last job for the F.B.I. and Amaya Wheeler. Then I would start a new life—no longer at Benson & Jones or doing weird undercover assignments. I would leave Benson & Jones and, for the moment, stay in my trailer near the Blue Palm, where I hoped Delores would soon return.

18.

My meeting in Savannah with Queenie, Charley, and Ed Baker had started well but ended with more confusion. I was finally free of my headaches, but my hands were still shaking.

Queenie noted with smile, "You know, Preston, you could use a few days in the sun."

Queenie was right. I needed a lot of sun.

And so, a few days later, I found myself in Queenie's small bungalow, tucked into a back alley on the waterfront, near the street where the carriage rides started.

Queenie had prepared a large filet of red snapper and a green salad. She suggested that we wait until after our meeting and then eat. I noticed that there was an extra place set at the table but didn't think too much about it. There was an ice-cold long neck Corona beer beside each plate, and a big bowl of chips.

Ed began by praising Queenie, Charley, and the missing, as usual, Evaldo for developing their brilliant idea of the cargo ship.

I was shocked to learn the truth: that there was, in fact, no real cargo ship, only what Queenie and Charley called a "ghost ship," They had simply floated the idea of a phantom ship to entice the local dealers. The Suárez brothers were the first to fall for this lie about a drug shipment. Then several small time local dealers fell too.

With F.B.I. guidance behind the scenes, Evaldo had set the dealers on fire with promises of an "El Dorado", built on the dream of profits from the giant capacity of a "cargo ship." He reassured them that it had been redesigned with secret holds built to hide the cocaine.

These outdated cargo ships were being replaced by the new giant container ships. A mere nineteen million was a bargain, and an indication of just how crazy the drug wars were becoming.

Charley added that Evaldo was still safely undercover and was regarded by the local dealers as the man with the secret weapon, a cargo ship whose capacity would dwarf the usual ways of smuggling cocaine.

I noted the casual mention of Evaldo's role in their plans. It was the first time any of them had ever bothered to fill me in on what, exactly, Evaldo's role was.

Charley's report was a tiny ray of light, but it still left too many unanswered questions in the dark. How long had Evaldo been cooperating with Ed Baker and the F.B.I.? Was he recruited before I went to Bolivia? Was Evaldo's first phone call inviting me to his home in Magdalena really part of the F.B.I.'s plan?

And what about his brother Chingo? In my mind, Chingo was always more than just an ambitious rancher desperate for money to save his cattle. Was all the Hauser family involved in drugs? I was never sure about their vague answers to my questions.

Ed Baker took over and went into more detail. He said the older cargo ships were loaded by cranes off the docks, lowering into the holds of the waiting vessels products from bananas to scrap metal. These ships were being replaced by the more efficient giant container ships. The container ship was a maritime revolution making the traditional smaller cargo ship almost obsolete and priced within the budget of a cartel.

The old cargo ships now on sale at bargain basement prices.

For smuggling purposes, one of these cargo ships could be bought and gutted, then redesigned so a false bottom could hold cocaine that could be sealed, and much harder to find if searched.

The price for one of these secondhand ships ranged from eighteen to twenty million dollars, a lot of money for all but a few of the big-time dealers like the Suárez cartel. But with the promise of a booming cocaine market, the dealers were willing to take the chance.

The cocaine dealers, buying from the small farmers working their plots of coca, could now safely offer them an almost limitless market for their product, guaranteed by the promise of the increased capacity of the cargo ships.

At this point, Ed turned to me and said, "Your job is to be our contact with Evaldo Hauser."

"You know why that's a bad choice," I said.

"If we had a better choice…" Ed shrugged, "but there is no one else with your inside contacts with the Hauser family."

"But I don't know about container ships and the current drug situation. Seeing those sides of beef on an isolated landing strip in the Beni doesn't make me an expert.

And Evaldo Hauser hasn't responded to me in months I am not sure about where I stand with him. Or him with me as a friend.."

"We're going to fix that," Ed said, with a finality that stopped my objections.

I felt I had been set up again, and that they were putting me in a situation where I couldn't say no. I was trapped "in dubious battle," faced with two choices. Both of them bad.

Queenie held up her hand. "I think I hear someone," and rushed to the door, which was hidden down a small hallway.

There was a delighted cry, and Queenie walked back with her arms wrapped around Evaldo Hauser.

"Here's our guest of honor."

Evaldo nodded hello to the others and walked over behind my chair and grabbed my shoulders.

"I'm sorry I turned my back on you in the marshes. At the time, I just couldn't risk blowing my cover."

I tried to say something, but couldn't.

On the one hand, I was angry at being kept in the dark, but at the same time I knew that it had probably been necessary. One slip in San Ramón and Arturo Suárez would have killed me himself. It was better I admitted that I had been kept in the dark.

I stood up and we embraced the way men do in the Beni with their arms wrapped around shoulders and slapping each other on the back, with a few que buena vertas" thrown in.

It was only then, as Evaldo slapped me on the back, that I began to feel myself relax. As if a heavy weight were being lifted off my shoulders.

I realized how much the thought of Evaldo's involvement with the Suárezes had affected me. Now I wanted to know how long Evaldo had been working with the F.B.I., and, why I was needed, with Evaldo's presence to give authenticity, credibility with the Suárezes.

I looked at the faces around the table and saw no sympathetic glances of understanding. I would have to settle for Evaldo and I being on the same side.

I looked at Agent Baker and said, "Why don't we finish our meal and then you can fill me in with the details."

We sat down to Queenie's delicious meal of red snapper and a fresh garden salad. I listened carefully as Ed and the others around the table outlined the dangers ahead for out small team.

Then, for the first time, I joined the conversation. Feeling that I actually belonged, I laughing as Ed Baker described my first meeting with Queenie and Charley.

I looked at Evaldo and began talking about what Carnival had been like in Magdalena and wondering how his mother and Chavela were doing. I told him about watching the bats with Padre Liborio.

I didn't mention King Momo and his warning me: "Don't come back." I needed time to verify how that disturbing message had reached me.

It was clear that Delores had known I was in Bolivia and sent me a clear warning in King Momo's message. Who would know about that message and how it was being used except Delores? Who told me, through King Momo, that my life was in danger, if not Delores?

Yet, she had said that she never wanted to see me again.

Or was it from someone else, warning me that the Suárezes had decided I should be killed?

Moving through these multiple levels of my life had a hypnotic effect on me.

Different times and places seemed to merge in a hallucinatory scene, where I could see my mother talking to Evaldo at the table in Queenie's apartment while Judge Talley was walking with me beside Arturo Suárez in San Ramón. I walked behind them across the heads of slaughtered cattle. Judge Talley kept repeating in a bored, ironic way to comfort my mother, "Preston wouldn't do that" over and over again.

Then I came out of it. I could feel someone pulling at my arm.

Queenie was standing beside my chair, holding a bottle of wine. She gave me a little pat.

I leaned back and took a deep breath.

Queenie looked at the others and said, "He's still with us."

I had passed out and the conversation at the table had moved on.

Ed Baker took a swallow of beer. He gave me a concerned look and asked, "Are you sure you are feeling better?"

"I'm okay, really," I reassured. "It's just the headaches. I start phasing out when the headaches first go away. I should have passed on that glass of beer."

I looked at Ed Baker. "How much did I miss?"

"You and Evaldo are meeting with me in the morning at nine., if you're up to it."

****

The next two weeks were frantic. Word of Evaldo's plan for a new and better way to bring in drugs to Savannah on the refitted cargo ship had spread.

Drug dealers began clamoring for news about how soon this new ship would be ready and how soon they could sign up, knowing it would revolutionize the market and heighten their profits.

Ed Baker was expecting the big cartels to make a move and either try to become a partner with Evaldo or else send a hit squad to take him out. I had to keep reminding myself that there was, in fact, no cargo ship—just rumors on the street about one.

All of this reminded me of D.H. Lawrence's poem "The Ship of Death." The few lines I could remember floated around in my head:

Have you built your ship of death, Oh have you?
Oh build your ship of death for you will need it,
For the voyage to oblivion awaits you.
And so, we waited for our phantom ship to dock.
And it would. We didn't know
then that it would come towing with it a deadly virus.

18.

I left the dinner at Queenie's feeling manipulated. All I needed to do was obey orders.

Ed Baker had told me that I was now working for the F.B.I., on an extended leave from my law firm.

Queenie and Charley were monitoring the Savannah waterfront and spreading wildly exaggerated rumors about the newly outfitted cargo ship's secret cargo holds for concealing drugs.

Evaldo and I would wait for the dealers on the street to contact us about the "ghost" cargo ship. We spent our days checking our throw-away phones as we sat at an outdoor table watching the flow of tourists move past us, ever-changing and always the same.

I recounted my experiences in Beni, from the tarantula in my room to the river trip to San Ramón to the oxcart turning over in the arroyo. I ended my story with Carnival and King Momo's message, using Delores's exact words telling me "Don't come back."

I wasn't sure if Evaldo was holding back information, but I decided to be as clear as possible. "You sent me that message from Delores, didn't you?"

At first Evaldo didn't say anything, then he nodded and said "Yes, I did, as a favor to Delores" He went on, Do you know why? I needed the exact words she used so you would believe the message, even if you were still not sure who sent it. I am a great admirer of your Delores, not in any personal way, not in any that would cause you to lose sleep. She has survived the worst and remains true to her mission—to help children trapped by war."

"How did you meet her? And did she know I was in danger? Or did you both know I was in danger, and you both wanted to warn me."

Evaldo looked bored, but also relieved. "Exactly. We moved in some of the same circles. She knew what I knew and maybe more. I just knew what I needed to know in order to bring in the profits to save our herds and ranches."

I was angry now, and ready to get my feelings out in the open at last.

"I think that's bullshit. I never lied to you. But as far as I can tell, you've never done anything but lie to me—from your bogus summons to help you with your dying father to your family's interest in taking control away from the Suárezes. You are a master at disappearances and secret operations."

For the first time, Evaldo seemed to lose his confidence.

"No, no, my friend. I admit that many lies are necessary. Remember, in law school that we read Plato on the lies necessary to protect the state. I think lies are often necessary to save a family."

"You haven't told one truth since your first phone call asking my help with your dying father–who evidently has recovered from that terminal condition was never mentioned after I got to Magdalena.

"And then, when you were supposed to meet me in Magdalena, you never showed. I heard Chingo—drunk, as usual—whisper to Arturo Suárez about a new secret plan that you were putting together. A plan to ship the drugs produced in Beni into outfitted cargo ship to Colombia to eventually dock here in Savannah.

"What was I to think except that you were in bed with Arturo Suárez, working hand in hand with, not against, the Suárezes when I saw you that evening out in the marshes? I know that you definitely saw me then near Tybee Island.

"Then when I saw you again with Ed Baker in the F.B.I. building, you didn't even acknowledge me those two times. I have to ask myself what happened to you, the man everyone trusted. Did you play both sides—Suárezes and the F.B.I.? Was it simply to make money for your family and your ranches, or was it to work with the F.B.I. to avoid being arrested? Were you playing both sides against each other?"

Evaldo looked at the ground for a long time as if studying something.

"I admit that it must have looked like betrayal to you. And yes, I was trying to play both sides. I wanted to throw a net over the Suárezes who have had us by the cajónes for years, taking the lion's share of the coca profits. I had to do business with Arturo Suárez or my entire family would have been wiped out."

I couldn't help saying, "Even if I became numero uno on the Suárez hit list?"

"I was desperate and needed time. You were there at San Ramón and saw the carcasses packed. I didn't want to put you in danger. The only person Arturo Suárez wouldn't kill is his strung-out brother Hernando.

"All of the big coca dealers are searching for new ways to transport their drugs to the States. The ranches in Beni make ideal landing strips for small planes. They can fly the cocaine from Beni to Brazil and then on to Colombia. Ships at

Cartagena can go straight north to the East Coast ports in the States—like here in Savannah.

"My idea was to spread the fake news of a cargo ship that was redesigned to hide drugs. It seemed the perfect solution. There will be no real ship, just a rumor. Only the drugs are real.

"Confiscated drugs that will be unloaded and stored in the Blue Palm sub-basement by the F.B.I., laying the trap for the Suárezes."

At last, I had the truth, if it was true, from Evaldo. The real plan was to arrest the Mexican Suarezes. I could see that this move would remove the competition from Hauser plan to market the cocaine they would produce. They would make profits and save their ranches.

Evaldo went on. "That's our plan. There is no real ship, only the rumor of one, loaded with drugs to be sold by the Suárezes to dealers in America."

I sat there, both furious and impressed. I would never have believed this delusional marketing scheme from anyone else, but I had met Arturo and Hernando Suárez at the landing strip in San Ramón and seen the fear in Chingo's eyes that was barely hidden under his gun-waving bravado.. I understood why Evaldo was desperate.

It was a brilliant strategy for attracting dark money later after the arrests—if all went according to the F.B.I plan.. It was hard for me to think that there was no real cargo ship, and that the entire plan depended on a ghost cargo ship that didn't exist.

I knew that Evaldo, like his brother Chingo, was trapped in this criminal economy. I hoped that he and Ed Baker could work together and end the Suárez control over the cocaine industry. The ghost ship idea might work to attract investors temporarily, but it seemed to me an impossible scheme. It would only work once, and then hope that, at the end, Arturo and Chingo would be in jail.

But, I thought, there is too much money to be made, and that the drug trade would soon recover. As long as there were coca growers out of reach in the high lands of South America, and desperate ranchers like the Hausers, the demand for drugs would never be satisfied.

I was in way over my head. It was a brilliant plan. As I understood it, it would get rid of the Suárez competition and later make money for Evaldo's family using the F.B.I.

Evaldo sat there waiting for my reaction. All I could think of just a simple summary from my point of view.

"O.K, I get it. You did not have a real choice. But at the same time, you were using me. I was set up, with no way to protect myself. You and Ed Baker kept me in the dark and sent me to Bolivia with no guarantees of me coming back alive. You and Baker are too careless when it's my ass on the line."

Evaldo gave me a long look. "Your Delores, the beautiful Delores, agreed. She didn't like the way we were using you either. She wouldn't cooperate unless we warned you. So before you left for Bolivia, we told her to tell you not to come back. And then we sent that very same message again, hidden in the rhyme King Momo read to you in Magdalena. It was good advice."

"None of your advice makes sense to me. Where was I supposed to not come back?""

Evaldo laughed. "We were working on finding you a new home. Look at it this way: It doesn't matter now since you made it back safely. Here you are, back in Savannah, having dinner with me."

"Is that supposed to make me feel better?"

"Of course. Just give her a call."

Evaldo looked out at the small ships at anchor, as if he had spoken from Mt. Olympus, and decreed my destiny.

"I've been trying to call her. The number in Switzerland isn't working."

"Not Switzerland. Her husband is the only one there."

"Then it has to be the Blue Palm."

"Try Satterwhites."

"Oh shit," I slammed my hand down on the table.

Evaldo leaned forward and almost whispering, "Calm down, my friend. Tell me, what's wrong with Satterwhites?"

"My mother is there with Judge Talley."

"So…?"

"Why isn't Delores staying at the Blue Palm with Khumar?"

"I just told you, he's in Switzerland."

Again, I couldn't believe this. "You mean she's left him?"

"She's here for just a couple of days."

"For what? Isn't Sandy Lefcourt taking care of things?"

"Yes, I think that's true."

"So why is Delores here?"

Evaldo rolled his eyes upward and slapped his forehead. "Idiot! She's here to see you."

I slumped bac in shock. Evaldo went on, "I am sorry that it might seem cruel to have delayed telling you where she is. Ann Lefcourt arranged it. Today is Tuesday.

You've got the rest of the day and tomorrow; then she flies back to Switzerland. So you have until noon on Thursday, and then you're back here at this table. I'll bring you up to date if anything big happens."

Evaldo hesitated, and then added, "And don't tell Ed Baker or anyone else where you are. That way you will have that time together."

I stood up, and tried to say something, but could only manage "Thanks."

Evaldo waved me away. "Time is passing."

I started to leave, but Evaldo said, "Wait, I almost forgot," and handed me a slip of paper. "It's her new cell phone number. Give her a call and tell her you're coming.

She's expecting you."

Outside, I sat in the car, listening as the phone rang. Then I heard her voice.

"Hello, Preston."

"I'm on my way. Listen, my mother and Judge Talley are at Satterwhites."

"I know. I'll be outside at the gate."

"Give me an hour and half."

"Yes... I'll be waiting."

I reached Satterwhites in record time. Delores seemed to fly over the ground and into my arms. We stood there, holding on to each other and swaying back and forth; both of us were so happy we cried.. I put her overnight bag in the back seat, and we were off.

Finally, she asked, "Where are we going?"

"To my place."

We drove on, with Delores leaning against me. Just as we drove past the exit to the Blue Palm Delores looked around: "Aren't we going to the hotel?"

"No. My place isn't at the hotel. I'm now in a trailer at Sunnyside Mobile Home Park."

We pulled in and drove around the sandy road that circled the court, slowly moving past the rundown trailers until we reached mine.

"This is it."

I looked at Delores, but all she said was "I've never seen anything like this."

"It looks better at night with some of the lights on."

Delores looked around and asked, "What kind of people live here?"

I took Delores by the hand, and we walked over and opened the front door of my trailer, and we went inside. My two fold-out sofas made a double bed. We undressed between kisses, and then pulled the covers over us.

Later, in the moonlight, we held each other and talked. She asked me if I had understood the warning about the danger I was in.

"No, I took don't come back as only personal, and that you wanted me out of your life. But I hoped that I could persuade you to let me stay."

"No, I do want you to leave. But not yet. I have things to tell you about my life, about things I wish were not true. And I am not talking the terrors of being a refugee child in a Syrian camp. I am talking about what Simon was drawn into during the last two years.

"It may look like he has become part of the drug trade, but that's not true. The cartels would have killed Simon if he had not cooperated and allowed the hotel to be a haven for the illegal drugs.

"As you know, the hotel is on a small island with one bridge connecting it to the mainland. It's ideally situated on the coast for ships to drop anchor offshore.

"My warning via King Momo did mean and still means we can never have a life together. We only have until Thursday."

I was determined to change her mind, to somehow make her understand that we could have a life together—for now and for always."

"I will wait for you, follow you, and protect you— whatever I have to do." I was cursing my helplessness as I said these words.

19.

We spent the next morning across the road at the beach. The sun was out and the waves just high enough to give us a real pounding. I didn't have a blanket, but I did have two large beach towels that I had never used. We spread them out and turned our backs to the sun.

Delores had a tube of sunscreen. I ran my hand up under her towel and felt the terrible scars on her back, ones that she had let me see at the Far Cottage a million years ago before she told me not to come back. Then she did my back. We were both moaning with pleasure as we felt ourselves relax.

Behind us was the highway that connected us to the world of the F.B.I. and the dark money of drug transactions and its dark money. In front of us, the blue expanse of the Atlantic made everything seem simple and easy, even though we knew that couldn't be the truth.

The phantom ship was on track to sail from Colombia to Savannah with its phantom cargo of cocaine paste. Queenie and Charley were watching, spreading lies about profits.

I felt trapped in this improbable scheme, and that we were all victims, including Delores and even her dying husband especially.

Delores and I were sitting on a narrow strand of white sand, believing for that morning at least, we could, like Don Quixote and Dulcinea, really live our impossible dreams.

I felt trapped by what she had told me the night before. I knew that she loved Simon, and that I couldn't even come close to saying what was obvious to me: Simon would not live much longer. I knew she owed her life to Simon, and would reject any proposal that sounded like 'Just wait until Simon dies and then we can get married.'

Ann Lefcourt had told me that Simon did not have long to live. Simon's health was deteriorating rapidly, and Delores would be hurrying back to Switzerland on Thursday.

So I would wait, saying nothing as I slowly massaged her back with more sunscreen.

I asked about Switzerland and the Swiss Alps. Delores seemed relieved, wanting to avoid thoughts of Simon's worsening condition.

She told me about Lake Constance and the river which flowed south past the small city, with its giant cathedral, before continuing on though Bavaria and into Switzerland, and finally emptying out into the Adriatic.

As she talked, her look of sadness slowly disappeared. "In Ulm," she said, "you can sit on a bridge at the confluence of a small stream with the Danube, and order freshly caught trout with your beer and a fresh salad. Einstein was born in Ulm, and it was the site of a big battle with Napoleon. Not only that, she said, but the Ulm Muenster boasted the highest church spire in the world." She summed all of this up for me, before saying "You Americans really have a lot to learn."

"What about motels and hot dogs."

Delores just laughed and said, "Hot dogs are just a degraded version of a good German sausage!"

This reminded us that we were getting hungry. We hurried back to my trailer, carrying my sunscreen and towels. We showered and in keeping with our morning conversation, we went hunting for a good German restaurant.

We found the Bavarian Haus which I hoped would earn Delores's seal of approval. The sausages erupted in our mouths when we bit into them. There was an amazing Baked Alaska for dessert. The beer was ice cold, American style, which was inauthentic gemütlich, but suited the hot Florida sun.

We took our time, talking about everything but the time, which lurked behind us like an enemy..

Finally, Delores said she needed a small wrap for Switzerland and we left to try the new shops that catered to the rich women from New Jersey and New York.

The boardwalk seemed endless. A summer shower rolled in off the ocean and we hurried into a nearby coffee shop. It seemed like a good time to talk, but just as they signaled that our iced coffee was ready, Delores got a vibrating hum on her cell.

She took the call and listened for a moment, then made a writing motion with her fingers. I handed her a pen and she took out her little tablet, writing quickly.

Simon had experienced a setback with rapid breathing and a spike in his temperature. It was serious.

Over the phone, Delores cancelled her motel reservations. Through her connections with Simon, she secured a flight from Dulles to Paris leaving late that afternoon. We would leave immediately, and I would drive her to the airport.

She looked at me and said there was nothing more she could do.

We did not finish our coffee. We hurried back to my trailer in silence. She packed her bag and we headed out.. Her flight would leave at nine the next morning.

As we drove, Delores told me what she and Simon had always agreed on, about what she would do when the time came. Delores stopped, but the meaning was clear; when Simon died, Delores would take over.

She said that from the very beginning, when Simon had found her hiding in a closet at the orphanage, he intuitively knew that she could carry out his life's work. As long as Simon was able, he would continue amassing as much money as possible for his humanitarian projects, doomed as they might be. When he was no longer able, Delores would take over. They would establish hospitals and homes for refugees in Europe and America.

"For the last five years, Simon has bought land in the United States, Canada, and Europe. All of it ready for development. In fact," Delores explained, "the Blue Palm renovations were not meant just to improve the old hotel and restore its former glory. It would become the headquarters for Simon's — and now my — international charities."

"What about Sandy Lefcourt? Does he know all these plans?"

"Yes, Sandy and Ann have agreed to stay on while I settle Simon's estate."

Delores paused, and said, "I think they want to make it permanent."

"And what about you? And me? What will happen to me in this grand scheme?"

"I hope that you will have the life you deserve. Getting tangled up in the drug trade isn't your fault. You will have to wait, but you can free yourself from it. Your friend Evaldo will need your help, but you need to have your own dreams, Preston. Not just what others want for themselves. You can channel your energies into constructive projects."

"What about Ras al-Ayn? Can you help those towns that are now rubble? Idlid, Aleppo, Latakia, Tartus, Damascus?"

"There are things that can still be saved."

But you don't think we can be saved. To be together?'"

"Of course, I do, but not in the way you are hoping.." She wept as she tried to speak, "And the doctors say I can never have children."

"We could adopt. And what about us, goddammit? We saw our future in the Far Cottage at least for a while and we were both happy. We both know that happiness in ourselves, our bodies, and our souls."

There was no answer. We did not even try to hide our tears from each other.

"Do you remember when I said, 'Don't come back,'?"

"How could I forget?"

"And now I'm saying this: You cannot come with me Ever."

"But I could be of some help with the legal issues."

Delores looked at me and we both were silent.

"Don't you see? You want what I cannot give?"

"What do you think I want?"

"Hope, Preston. You say impossible things that are not hopeful. Ed Baker says you're number one on the Suárez hit list."

I slowed down and started looking for a place to pull over.

"How do you know that?"

"I know more than you think I do. Simon and Evaldo do too. Didn't Evaldo tell you? I helped Ed put together the King Momo message he sent you in Bolivia."

There was a rest area ahead and I started to slow down.

"Keep going," Delores said.

I drove on, sick at heart and hardly able to see the highway.

"Should I drive? You're going to kill us both."

"Freud says there are no accidents."

At the airport, I put her luggage on the sidewalk. She stood in front of me and said, "This is goodbye."

"Not yet."

"Don't follow me to Switzerland," she ordered before grabbing her bag and turning away. Then she was gone, disappearing toward the departure gate.

I remembered the message over Dante's Gates of Hell, "Abandon all hope, ye who enter here," but I was not allowed to enter, so I was hopeless before I even got through the gate. Somehow these words of the great epic of sorrow seemed all wrong.

I was, watching as Delores vanished in the crowds. Unlike Orpheus, she did not look back.

If I couldn't follow her, where should I go?

I felt I had been turned into a stone, blindly rolling forward, crushing everything in my path.

Outside, driving back toward the Blue Palm, I could feel my despair settle over me and a cold anger set in.

This was what death must be like when everything in life is over, I thought. I felt like a zombie, one of the undead who could speak but would never be heard.

Once when I was six, my mother held my face up to the old mirror in our hall and said, "This is you. Don't cause any trouble. Do what you are told." And so, I did—in school and under the judge's rules. The only time I rebelled was when I declared that I was majoring in English, because I loved the lines from the great writers. I loved Hamlet's saying, "I have of late lost all my mirth." I know now how the poor guy felt.

The judge had sneered at paying for my English major, but continued to pay my tuition only if I went to law school. My mother remained silent, and it was clear that I was causing her trouble. I waited for others to tell me what rules I must follow.

I stopped at my mother's house in Clover, knowing that she and the judge were still at Satterwhites, hiding from the virus. The house was empty, but the letter from Uncle Virgil was there.

Now I needed his money, but I didn't remember where it was—in what bank. I was running on empty and had used my reserves from going to Bolivia. I would have to confront my mother and find out where the money from Uncle Virgil was. Or reread the letter from him. I thought that he had put the account number and the bank in it, and I had forgotten.

I realized why Uncle Virgil had left money for me. I had been eleven when my mother had served me the Blue Jays. The terrible scene washed over me again. It was his unexpected sympathy that I had forgotten and now remembered.

He had said, "Louise, I had a rough time as a boy, leather belts, fists, locked out of the house, but never was I made to eat dead birds carefully prepared and roasted by my mother. What you did to that boy, your own son, was cruel. I don't know why he ate what you put on his plate, every bite. Then I saw him run out back and vomit. Maybe this money will help him now."

20.

The street talk in Savannah was alive with rumors about the "ghost" cargo ship headed for the Blue Palm. The plan was in motion. The Suárezes would then be busted, if things worked according to Ed Baker's plan.

It would be a perfect storm of arrests. Best result: a big promotion for Baker, money for Evaldo's family's ranches, and, for me, freedom from the connections with Bolivia, drugs, and their corresponding danger.

But, when it was all over, I knew that, for me, this storm of good outcomes would only end with me ending up alone at the mobile home park, wrecked and marooned by the loss of Delores.

At the same time, I needed to confront my mother about another ghost: a promise of the inheritance from Uncle Virgil. Uncle Virgil had entrusted my mother with money meant for me, but where was it?

I couldn't help but wonder, Is this the way the world works, on false promises and secrets? Ghost ships, criminal profits heartbreak,, arrests, gunfire? So far, the answer seemed to be a resounding "Yes!"

My mother had kept this money a secret. It wasn't until I read uncle Virgil's letter that I had found hidden in her bedroom that I learned what he had done for me.

I needed to know if the money had already been spent, or if my mother had saved it for me as the letter clearly intended her to do. And, if it had been saved, was it in my name in a bank? And, if so, where?

I dreaded going back to Satterwhites to see my mother and the judge. Unless I had access to the money from Uncle Virgil, I would soon be out of cash, with no way to pay my rent, even at Sunnyside. I was still on a 'temp' status at both Benson & Jones and the F.B.I.

My fantasy of independence had faded. I would get a lump sum payment when my assignments were finished. I knew the judge would be outraged after learning that I planned to be resign from Benson & Jones, since his recommendation was responsible for my being hired.

If I were foolish enough to say that I needed the money, my mother would have to face the reality of either handing Uncle Virgil's money over to me or admitting that she had spent over the years.

I remember Delores saying that she had seen my mother and Judge Talley sitting at a table at Satterwhites. I could imagine the scene there. The judge would have his usual sullen look of impatience while my mother sat at the other end of the table, her face in profile, with the expressionless stare of a cameo, and her archaic smile like a Mona Lisa.

I could easily imagine the dialogue. They were probably arguing about what to order for dinner. My mother would wait for the judge to make up his mind.

She would suggest something from the menu, and he would say, "We ordered that last night." He would then add something like, "You're losing your mind, Louise.

You really need to see a doctor."

****

The next morning at Sunnyside, the owner knocked at the door of my trailer just as I was finishing my shower.

"There's a message for you," he yelled.

I guessed it was a bill, since my rent was past due, and I yelled back, "I'm on it!" and waited.

There was no response.

I looked out the window. The person seemed to be sliding something under my door, then straightened up and began walking away. This supercharged my resolve, which had been eroding, to leave for Satterwhites.

I finished dressing and opened the door to pick up the envelope and saw Delores's handwriting.

I decided not to read it until I had Uncle Virgil's money in hand and could buy the ticket for Switzerland. I would find Delores and persuade her to come back with me.

I headed out for Satterwhites, my car radio blaring what seemed an appropriate country song about a dead mother.

"I was standing on a corner,
On a dark and cloudy day,
When I saw that hearse come rolling
For to carry my mother away."

I wasn't sure what I would find at Satterwhites. Would my mother and the judge deny that Uncle Virgil's letter had been left in a box in her room.

I stopped for gas and a ham biscuit, hoping that at least one of my credit cards had not maxed out. Again, the gods of invisible money were kind and I drove away before my luck could change.

That's twice, I thought to myself: First the trailer park owner giving me a reprieve on the rent, and then my credit card keeping me afloat for another day. How long would my luck hold?

My mind went blank until I realized I was getting close to Satterwhites. I put away all my thoughts about Delores and tried to focus on the upcoming talk with my mother.

Would she and the judge try to justify what they had done by keeping me in the dark about my inheritance?

I remembered a phrase from my old second year Latin class, when Caesar made the decision to cross the Rubicon, he said, "alea iacta est" (The die is cast). He saw his invasion of Rome as the end of the Republic that had lasted five hundred years. It was a throw of the dice. Feeling better, I could only add, "And let them fly high."

I gave the guard at Satterwhites the judge's name, and, after a brief call, he handed me a map with a circle around the judge's bungalow.

"Just follow the signs," he said curtly and waved me on.

I drove through a landscape designed for the very rich. The "bungalows" would have been mansions or villas in most real estate brochures. I looked for signs that I could recognize from my last visit years ago.

I could only identify the lake, and as I drove past it, there was a sign saying "The Deep Dive" restaurant. I turned into the drive that circled around in front of the restaurant and slowed down.

Satterwhites office had been replaced, but I could see that the submerged dining room had been kept, retaining its sinister look of floating underwater. I wondered what had happened to Lem Satterwhite, Aunt Sally and her daughter Aster, who had brought me a cake and remembered the judge's "wife" with blonde hair.

I pulled back out on the main road. The judge's bungalow was nearby.

I rang the bell at the front door, and the judge opened it immediately as if he had been standing behind it. He had an impatient 'waiting to attack' look on his face.

"Your landlord from the mobile home park called."

"Yes, I took care of it this morning."

I wanted to ask the judge how my landlord knew how to reach him, but decided to stay focused. The judge looked surprised.

"It wasn't about your rent. It was about a registered letter. I told him to slip it under your door."

I felt the unread letter from Delores burning a hole in my pocket.

"Oh! Yes, I have the letter."

This seemed to satisfy the judge. He stepped back and motioned me inside.

"Your mother has been worried about you."

"It's been a busy time."

As I walked past him, I felt the judge give me suspicious glance.

My mother was sitting on a large light green chaise lounge and looked up and waved me over.

"Hello, dear. I'm so glad you came."

She held out her arms. I leaned over and kissed her cheek. I could smell the gin.

I looked around and asked, "How do you like the new Satterwhites?"

My mother nodded. "It's quite a change, isn't it?"

Before I could answer, she started coughing with a dry, rasping sound.

"I'll bring you some water," the judge said.

I waited until the judge disappeared and then said to my mother, "I found Uncle Virgil's letter on your dresser."

I was expecting anger, or some defensive attempt at an explanation. Instead, my mother smiled.

"Yes," she said, "the judge has already arranged to put the money in an account in your name. We both think it's the best thing to do. We were planning to give it to you earlier, but then you left for Bolivia. I hope you're not upset."

I didn't expect that.

"No, I'm not upset." I said, feeling thrown off balance. "That's good to hear."

The judge came back with the glass of water. "I guess she told you about your inheritance?"

"Yes, she did."

"And you're all right with it?"

We were all silent.

Then the judge added, "Let's agree to talk about this later. Your mother really needs to rest."

He walked me to the door.

"Your account is at the Florida National Bank in Clover." He handed me a little plastic bag. "I put ten thousand in checking and the rest in savings. Your bank books are in this bag, with the usual stuff from the bank. The manager is J. T. Harlow. I'll call ahead. By the time you get home you can open your account and write a check."

I drove back to Sunnyside feeling like an orphan or a refugee who had been abruptly given his passport, which, I thought, wasn't too far from the truth. I put off stopping at the bank.

To inherit money and to have lost Delores left me paralyzed. I needed to read her letter, which might offer hope of some kind.

I don't remember the drive back to the Sunnyside Mobile Home Park. I was in limbo, but with a chance of finding an exit to a world I could pay rent in without working for Benson & Jones.

Back in my mobile home, I opened a bottle of whiskey, poured a double shot, and sat down with the letter in front of me.

I had delayed opening it, dreading to but hoping for Delores's words to offer me some reason to live. I drained the glass and reached for the letter in my pocket.

There was a loud banging on my door.

"Hey, Honey! Are you in there?" It was the always-alert Angel, the wife of the Sunnyside's owner.

"Yes, I'm in here. Go away."

"I need to talk to you. Real Bad."

I got up and opened the door. Angel was standing there, dressed in her usual too tight shorts and a tee shirt knotted at the waist. The rumor was that she was about thirty-five but looked sixty, with meth teeth and years of tanning which had turned her skin to leather.

"How bad is it?"

"I'm not sure. Some people are looking for you."

"Did you get a name?"

"No, but two of them were dressed in clown suits. The driver, who was not a clown, said his name was Baker and that it was important. They were fucked-up crazies."

"Those are my three friends from the F.B.I." I knew I was saying too much but did not care.

"You must be in a shitload of trouble," Angel said, giving me the leering grin of someone who has had her darkest suspicions confirmed.

"No."

"Are you short on cash?"

I was about to go into my usual routine of 'I'll have the money for you in the morning,' but then I remembered Uncle Virgil and Florida National Bank and started laughing.

"No, actually, I am rich."

Angel grinned, "If you say so. Just have the rent money in the morning or you'll have to move your ass out of our park."

She waved and added "Bye, Sugar," then turned and walked away.

I went inside and refilled my glass. The letter was there waiting. I started to pick it up but decided to wait until I finished my drink. This was a bad decision because that drink was followed by another, and then another, and another.

A few hours later I was still sitting at the table, and Delores's letter was unopened. I had finished the whiskey and had started on Coors Lite. I reached out for the letter but lost my balance and fell off the bed.

I woke up the next morning somehow on the sofa. The unopened letter still in front of me.

As I stood up, my stomach heaved. I headed for the bathroom and threw up. I forced myself to take a cold shower, and then changed to fresh clothes.

I put the letter back in my pocket and went out to find a restaurant that served what I needed: A Bloody Mary with Worcestershire sauce, a squeeze of lemon, salt and pepper, and a raw oyster dropped in for good measure, plus a double shot of vodka.

My head began to clear as I walked back to my mobile home; questions with no answers were spinning around in my head. Where had Uncle Virgil's money come from? Why was Judge Talley being so cooperative? And why was my mother, who had roasted Blue Jays to teach me some kind of lesson, concerned about me? What would the letter from Delores say, and would it be something that I could live with?

And another important question: What would happen at the Blue Palm? I remember hearing it discussed as a possible site for the delivery or storage of the drugs from Cartagena for the Suarezes, but were these real or imagined drugs brought in a phantom ship?

My work with Ed Baker and his C.I.'s in clown suits from Savannah was a "known-known operation," with many questions that probably had answers but not ones I knew. I was not in the Need To Know group.

By now, the ghost ship from Cartagena must be approaching the coast of Florida.

Ed Baker, Queenie, Charley, and maybe Evaldo would be getting ready to make a move, but how and where? The dice were about to be thrown and real money was on the table, probably by heavy hitters like Arturo Suárez, not knowing they were betting on a ghost ship with only imagined cargo.

I knew Baker would soon be back to see me.

I forced myself to finally read Delores's letter.

It destroyed me and my hope of being with her again, but it offered a poisoned gift as compensation—she had deeded the Blue Palm Hotel jointly to me, Ann, and Sandy Lefcourt. We would be equal partners.

Delores hoped that I would understand her gift. But instead, I was sickened, as if again, I were eating the Blue Jays served to me by my mother. How could a hotel be compensation for losing Delores, as if we were talking mortgages and investments?

I almost collapsed on the floor. She was not reversing her command "Don't come back" as I had hoped. Instead, she echoed it, re-enforced it. She went on about her deep need to help the orphans in Idlib.

I finished the letter in absolute despair. The bonds between us were broken. I was sure I would never see her again.

For a few moments, I hated her and her gift of the old hotel. I cursed them both, and that gave me temporary relief. Orphans and refugees had taken my place.

The next morning, I was able to force myself to slow down and read her letter again. The first two lines about her writing material—the Blue Palm stationery and Simon's pen—seemed foolish and obscure at first. But finally, when I reached the part where she said that Simon had deeded the hotel to me, Sandy and Ann, my only two friends, I understood why she had mentioned the stationary and the pen. As the new owner, I, too, she said, would soon be writing on hotel stationery and using an expensive new fountain pen.

My Dear Preston,

I am writing to you on the Blue Palm stationery with the fountain pen Simon gave me because I know how you dislike email.

I also know how much I love you and always will. We will always have our love beyond the Far Cottage. But I must remind you why we must live separate lives. You, of course, will not understand this for a long time, and I wish that it did not have to be this way.

There are two things that may help you understand—two realities that, to repeat, will take you a long time to accept. First, as I told you earlier, the doctors have told me that I can never have a child. You deserve a family, one that you will love and devote yourself to. I need a child, children, and I can hear the orphans in my country crying. The Anadolou Orphanage tries to offer refuge to the children, victims of a failing effort to end the cruel government of Bashar al-Assad. Yet the brave efforts of those who work with the displaced and suffering are pitifully inadequate, and I can offer very little in proportion to the need. Simon's support has helped greatly, but now, I must continue this work.

The second thing you need to know is more about Simon—his character, his soul, his vision. He has known about our love for each other all along. He has encouraged and supported it. Our hours together were his gift. He did not feel deceived or betrayed. In fact, he rejoiced, (his word), in our fulfillment. He knew he was dying and our love enriched his life. He defies tradition—its despair, jealousy, revenge, punishment. To make this clear, he has deeded half the Blue Palm to you and half to Sandy and Ann Lefcourt, with the request that you retain Sandy and Ann Lefcourt as managers.

I know that this news shocks you beyond words. It does not shock me because I know Simon's transcendent spirit: to see the good, regardless of circumstance. His is a rare gift to you and me—to the world. Accept his generosity as a sign of his recognition that you and I have a right to love each other. You know the history of how he rescued me from the ruins of Idlib. With the gift of the hotel, he is paying tribute to the greater gift of love that poets have celebrated.

Simon hired you on Ann's recommendation and he watched you care for all that the old hotel needed: the lawns, pools, cottages, guests, staff, kitchens, everything. You were always there, and, I think more importantly for Simon, I had chosen you. Without knowing it, you became his son, in a way. You and I will always have the Far Cottage.

Delores

****

Days later, after reading Delores's letter, I overheard a woman at the mobile home park talking about a man who had died; how others had loved him and how he always seemed to see the best in everyone. And I thought that if it had been me who had died, who would have noticed? Would anyone have remarked on the value of my life?

Others seemed to find love; I had thought that only Delores understood my real feelings, and that only Delores understood my sense of not belonging anywhere.

I was sure that Delores felt that the gift of the hotel would create a space for me to become connected and involved in life. But I could not accept the gift.

She may have meant for me to reach out to others and find a new life. To refuse to live the life of a stranger that denied any connection to humanity. To outgrow my passionate but necessary impulses.

She meant for the gift of the hotel to draw me toward life. Somehow, she was convinced that this would begin to rescue me as she herself had been rescued.

And now, deep inside me, something turned, and I became convinced of one thing: Delores was wrong. I wanted her to come back to me. I did not want a hotel.

What had happened to bring an old hotel into my ruined life? Was the reason for this gift really telling me a truth about my life, or was it just a truth filtered through Delores's obsessions to help herself?

That evening at Sunnyside Mobile Home Park, I felt that I was lost in the abyss, trying to find my way out. To me, there was one simple question that would have clarified everything:

Why didn't Delores just sell the hotel and use the money to support the orphans? Was I really another poor orphan who needed to be rescued?

Yes, she was a St. Teresa in her devotion to the orphans, but she was also the opposite, a Medea whose gift could kill. Wasn't she offering the poisoned robe just as Medea had given her husband's new bride such a gift? She may have meant to offer me reparations for my suffering?

My anger grew darker, and I could feel her iron hand of control, the same hand that had co-signed the deed giving me the hotel. It was Delores who used others—including me—to satisfy her needs. It was her vision of the world that could not be altered.

Again, I heard the echo of her words "Don't come back." I knew now that she really meant it, but not to protect me. We had not had a lovers' quarrel, where we would return to each other after the storm. The Far Cottage was not our Lovers' Retreat.

What had happened? No one gives away a hotel worth a few million to help a person she never wants to see again, a person she had said to be disconnected from life.

Outside my mobile home I heard a car slow down and stop.

I looked out my window.

Ed Baker was sitting in his car. Ed didn't get out but simply rolled his window down and said, "Things are beginning to happen. We can meet at Queenie's place tomorrow. Queenie will call about the time."

The next morning after taking care of Uncle Virgil's gift, I again found myself heading toward Savannah. This time with money from Uncle Virgil and a hotel to be managed. I was racked by the surging winds of grieving, loss, and fear.

22.

I had always been amazed by the Savannah waterfront.

As far as I could tell, the city had been built on a high hill at the confluence of the Savannah River and the Atlantic Ocean.

The waterfront was lined with shops and restaurants. You could sit outside at your table and watch an enormous freighter suddenly appear, gliding silently past and so close you could read the print on the side of the ship.

Now, I was on my way to Queenie's apartment again and thinking about my last meeting with Ed Baker and the gang. I recalled the late-night trip that ended at the river marshes around Tybee Island, where we watched the small fishing boat as it disappeared into the darkness. I had thought I saw Evaldo, a shrouded figure standing on the deck. All of this had filtered through the red film of another attack of my cluster headaches and the memories of my friendship with Evaldo.

Now Delores was gone, and in the rubble of my life, I had thought briefly that I might still have a job with Benson & Jones. I had completed two assignments for them: a preliminary assessment of potential witnesses for a murder trial at a community college, and a trip to Bolivia to assess the cocaine traffic in the remote state of the Beni.

All of this changed with Delores's gift of the hotel. Now I found myself half owner of an old hotel on Florida's gold coast.

In addition, the inheritance from Uncle Virgil made me recall the terrible meal of the roasted Blue Jays served by my mother at his table. Paradoxically, the hotel gift sent me deeper into my depression, which made me see that I needed the money. I remained unable to see my mother as the beneficent figure she wanted me to see her as.

My life roared into overdrive. And yet this hyper-speed had the strange effect of slowing things down. I had only recently returned from the Beni, where a missionary floated by in a tree on the flooded Itonomas River, and an oxcart had turned over, spilling me and three women across the bottom of a dry arroyo in the middle of the night. Then there had been the skeletal figure of King Momo, using Delores's words to warn me not to come home.

In the bizarre, artificial world of Florida, all of these moments seemed as if they had happened years ago. But now there was something big that kept me connected to them all: the ghost drug ship and Evaldo's plan.

Judge Talley had scoffed at reports of drugs delivered to the Blue Palm, and said, "Grow up, Preston, and do your job: Finish the report about your trip to Bolivia." Then, in a moment of cover your ass self-reflection, he added "Let me take a look at it before you turn it in."

"I'm almost finished. The Suárez brothers are enraged that the Hausers, my sometime friends, want to control the coca business. Their hired guns don't fool around.

It's like I'm in a desert with no trees to hide behind."

"Preston, there are lots of trees in Florida."

"Not one big enough to give me cover."

"Go meet with your F.B.I. contact, Ed Baker, and have a talk."

"I will, tomorrow."

"There you go!" the judge said in a jovial dismissive voice. "The F.B.I. won't put you in any kind of risky situation. You're a civilian. They're just using you because of your trip to Bolivia for the law firm and your connection to the Hausers. You make the F.B.I. plan to organize a large-scale drug bust on the Floridian coast seem plausible."

Out of some instinct for self-preservation, I did not tell the judge that I now owned several million dollars' worth of property—half of a hotel on the coast of Florida.

The next day I found myself knocking on the door of Queenie's apartment at two in the afternoon. Queenie opened it and gave me a quizzical smile.

"Preston, how nice." She seemed surprised, which I felt was not a good sign.

"Where is everybody?"

The smile vanished. "Oh, didn't they tell you? We're not meeting until four."

"Baker told me it was set for two."

"That was changed to four." Queenie gave a little explanatory kind of laugh.

"I guess somebody forgot to tell me." I had brought a six pack of Corona long-necks and held it up. "Why don't we talk about it inside?"

Queenie hesitated. "Well…. Sure…Why not?" Then she stepped back and opened the door. "You pour the beer and I'll get the chips."

"Sounds good."

"Oh and pour mine in a glass. I like a good head on my beer. It tickles my nose."

"No problem."

I watched her disappear down the hall. No surprise that I had not been told about the change in the time for the meeting. I was forgettable, as Delores and Queenie had both said about my face, but at the same time, I was now seen as a "key player."

I wondered if that had anything to do with my now owning half of the Blue Palm Hotel, the eventual destination, for the ghost ship to deliver the drugs. I couldn't help feeling that owning half of a hotel did not help my situation.

In a few minutes Queenie returned. I pointed to her beer sitting on the counter.

"Still lots of head."

Queenie looked at her cell phone and settled in a chair. "Ed sends his apologies for the mix-up about the time." She smiled and lifted her glass. "Here's to good luck."

"I hope so."

Queenie's eyes narrowed. "Are you worried about something?"

"Nothing major," I said. "Just trivial things like running for my life and getting shot."

Queenie leaned forward and gave me a serious look. "We would never put you in any real danger."

"It's comforting to know that, but it would be nice if you or Ed could tell me exactly what measures are in place to keep that from happening. I know the Suárez brothers.

We were San Ramón together. I walked to town with Arturo after watching his coca paste being loaded on his plane, and his crazy brother inciting a mob to hate the gringos. As the saying goes, they know my name."

"I'm sure that they still believe you can be trusted."

"Why? Arturo Suárez doesn't trust anybody, and his brother enjoys killing people."

"They trust your friend, Evaldo. He talked to Hernando Suárez a few days ago.

Hernando asked about you."

"Hernando Suárez is an insane killer. Even his brother says so. The last time I saw Hernando he was spraying buckshot over the heads of a cheering crowd."

Queenie's eyebrows lifted. "That must have been terrifying."

"You had to be there."

Queenie leaned forward. "I need to tell you: Hernando Suárez is here in Savannah as we speak, waiting for our ghost ship to come in with what they see as 'their' cocaine."

I leaned back in my chair, trying to control my impulse to yell. "If Hernando Suárez is here, then I'm a dead man!"

Queenie continued. "Hernando isn't that interested in you now. He's only interested in his cocaine."

"And what will he do when he finds out that 'his' cocaine and the ship that brought it don't actually exist? That the ship does not exist?"

Queenie looked at me and smiled. "Sure it does. It's already been unloaded."

"Where?"

"It's in the sub-basement of the Blue Palm. You know, the hotel you now own.

Sandy and Ann Lefcourt are cooperating with us. Even Judge Talley is helping. The cocaine was brought to the hotel and unloaded a couple of nights ago. On a real ship."

I tried to process this nightmare report. I jumped up and almost lost my balance.

"I don't believe it! Why wasn't I told? And how did it get here from Cartagena?"

"Plans get changed. Just calm down and listen. There was no ship in Cartagena.

It's a 'ghost ship', remember? The people with the Georgia Drugs and Narcotics Agency have seized tons of cocaine in ships coming into Savannah over the last six months."

Queenie paused to do air quotes. "They 'lent' us some of that 'product' to store in the sub-basement at the Blue Palm. We'll tell Arturo and Hernando the cargo ship with their cocaine arrived and that you and Evaldo Hauser are working together. You, of course, had agreed to store it at the Blue Palm for a fee. Let's say ten percent."

"This is crazy; using confiscated drugs to set a trap at the Blue Palm won't work.

The. Suárezes will know I set them up. I'll be number one on their hit list. I don't want to end up as collateral damage in one of your reports. Why am I the one in the dark?

Evaldo knew, and it sounds as if everyone else did too. Delores? Judge Talley? As far as I can tell, I'm the only one who could be paying with his life. You could at least have told me when the real drugs came in from the F.B.I. and that the drugs would be stored at the hotel!"

"It's already come and gone. It's a ghost ship, remember?"

"Since the drugs are in my hotel now, why wasn't I consulted?"

"Sandy Lefcourt tried multiple times to reach you. We couldn't wait any longer.

Besides, how could you object? You're still on the F.B.I. payroll."

I fell back into a chair. "Do you have a safe house nearby?"

"You won't need one. The Suárezes are arranging for their people to pick up the cocaine tomorrow night. They already have three panel trucks lined up.

"We'll be waiting with a F.B.I. team, along with a team from Georgia Drug and Narcotics Agency. We'll drop the hammer after the trucks are loaded."

Queenie paused, and then added, "Arturo asked specifically for you, Preston, to be there so he can thank you. It seems he now thinks of you as an old friend."

"That message comes from Arturo, not from Hernando... I met him at San Ramón, and believe me, Arturo doesn't trust anybody. I never spoke with Hernando. He was stoned out of his mind that night in San Ramón."

"No problem. In order to reassure Hernando, Evaldo will be standing next to you."

"So, Hernando can kill us both?"

Queenie stood up. "I need another beer." She gave me a look and said, "How about you?"

I could only manage a strangled, "Sounds good."

I leaned my head back against a pillow and closed my eyes, listening as she opened two bottles. I suddenly felt I needed something stronger. "Make it a beer with a shot of vodka."

By the time Ed Baker and Charley arrived I was on the sofa, mumbling songs I remembered from Carnival in Magdalena.

I heard the three of them hold a conference at the door, with Queenie whispering and Ed nodding his head as he looked over at me sprawled on the sofa.

Ed came over and sat down. "So, Queenie says you're worried."

I held up my empty bottle of beer and said, "Alcohol is good, even if it sets off my cluster headaches."

Ed took the bottle out of my hand. "Queenie has an extra bedroom. Why don't you spend the night here?"

Before I could answer, Ed and Charley lifted me by my shoulders and began walking me down the hall. I began singing something like "The Suárezes are coming, ta da ta da, /we're all going to die, ta da ta da." Then everything went dark until the next morning.

I woke up with a splitting headache, but thankfully, the clusterfucks had not returned. It was only an everyday hangover headache that I could deal with.

The next day, back at my trailer, and against what was left of my judgment, I answered Delores's letter. I decided to use a ball point pen and paper torn out of an old notebook.

I had to steel myself to keep from saying that I would always love her, even knowing that she was part of a plan that could kill me.

I could not bring myself to write 'Dear Delores' or 'My Darling Delores.'

Delores,

I can hardly hold this ball point pen as I try to write to you on notebook paper. I will try to get your address from the Lefcourts. I have come to learn things I should have known or should have been told about: The use of the Blue Palm as the epicenter for the drug delivery as part of the F.B.I.'s plan is beyond my comprehension, especially since you have deeded half of the hotel to me.

Why involve me in this deadly operation? You must have known that a criminal scheme was underway and that such a plan would endanger me.

Evaldo said that you were the most beautiful woman he had ever seen. Knowing Evaldo as I do I wonder if there was more to this statement than just an appreciation of your beauty.

Instead of my continuing to suspect betrayal and maybe infidelity, I would rather focus on what the drug money will mean for you. I don't know your plan to help the suffering families of Idlib. I also know about Evaldo's dream for that money would be used to breed a type of cattle better suited for the Beni's tropical environment. I don't know what deal he has worked out either.

But I must ask if Simon knew his hotel would be a crime site for bringing drugs into the voracious American market? Did Simon want his philanthropy to be funded by the sale of cocaine? I know the F.B.I.'s plan is to catch the Suárezes using the Blue Palm, but things can, and often, go wrong. Did Simon know people might get killed?

I beg you to let me know your thoughts. I fear that I am expendable in the F.B.I.'s plan. I am useful because I own the hotel, thanks to Simon and you. That is close to being 'forgettable' as Queenie once said about me. When the F.B.I. knew that I was the owner of the Blue Palm, I became even more valuable since I was more useful. And more expendable. I have been wondering why King Momo echoed your words "Don't come back," words that could only have come from you. This wasn't just a warning about the dangers in Bolivia, and it wasn't only about the drug shipment plan for the Blue Palm. You didn't want me to know that you were involved in the drug operation. So, why did you deed me part of the hotel if you were so concerned about me? Were you trying to clear your conscience? Doesn't my owning the hotel make me guilty instead of you?

I feel that the Suárez brothers have a bullet with my name on it, even if the drug deal goes through without a hitch. Your own connection to all this may be peripheral, or entirely altruistic in your motives to help refugees and especially children in war-torn countries.

Maybe not. But since the drugs are stored in the Blue Palm, it may end up getting me shot. Because of what seemed to me, at least, to be a genuine love at the Far Cottage, I think you owe it to me to tell me what was really going on.

—Preston

22.

I was scheduled to meet in the F.B.I. Building's conference room—the same building where I left my 'I Quit' note—with Evaldo and the F.B.I. team at 6:30am, three mornings after the "arrival" of the ghost ship. Of course, there was no ship, but the drugs were real, the ones seized in raids by the F.B.I. and "planted" in the sub-basement of the Blue Palm Hotel. Ed Baker had warned us that we needed to be on time. Our group—Ed Baker, Evaldo, Queenie, Charley, and I—would have a "team" breakfast and then go over the "plan."

I tried to take notes to make sure I understood what my role would be, but by the end, I was left with a list of unanswered questions and things I didn't understand.

I had come to the meeting after a night of nightmares, featuring tarantulas and Chingo's drunken gunfire at San Ramón, and brought with me a foreboding of impending disaster.

Evaldo had not shown up.

There was a plate of sausage biscuits and glasses of orange juice, with the usual Government Issue coffee, warming in an enormous urn. My hands were shaking as I tried to hold my cup and saucer as I sat down.

Ed started the meeting by summarizing how the real drugs, confiscated by the Savannah Port Authority had been bagged and placed in the sub-basement of the Blue Palm. They would be brought up and loaded by the Suárez crew, dressed as hotel maintenance workers, into the panel trucks waiting in front of the hotel. The drug deal would be completed when Arturo handed over the cash payment to Evaldo. This would be recorded by the hidden cameras that had been mounted at key points. These The recordings would be the smoking guns leading to the arrest of Arturo and Hernando Suárez.

I noticed there was nothing in this plan that would fund Delores's work in Syria.

Baker handed out a map of the hotel's external grounds, then another map with the interior plans of the hotel's exits, elevators on the main floor, and the sub-basement.

His tone was brisk, confident, and intended to be reassuring.

The success of the plan, which he never called a drug bust, depended on the Suárez's trust in Evaldo Hauser and I. We were the only two of our team who were not professional law enforcement officers and had no training in such trivial matters such as how to stay alive during a drug raid.

I wanted to ask, as the new half-owner of the Blue Palm hotel, why no one had asked for/demanded my permission to have a major drug raid there but thought better of it. It was too late.

Baker went on to discuss one of the major unanswered questions about the F.B.I.'s plan: What would happen if, with his brilliant criminal mind, Arturo Suárez asked "When did your ship arrive with the drugs?" Would he be suspicious when we said that the ship had arrived several days earlier and then departed for its home port? And that all he needed to do was to bring the drugs up from the where they were being stored in the Blue Palm's sub-basement and load them into the Suárezes' trucks?

The F.B.I. was banking on the smooth transition from the hotel sub-basement to waiting the trucks. The fact that there were real drugs being loaded would convince the Suárezes that the operation was going as planned.

On the other hand, I wondered what if Arturo asked, "Why wasn't he immediately informed when the ship from Cartagena docked in Savannah?" All Baker could say was that Evaldo and I, standing alone out front, would have to deal with that question if Arturo asked it.

The Suárezes were scheduled to arrive just before dark later tonight. The deal could be concluded and the money given to Evaldo after the drugs were loaded into the panel trucks. While the exchange was taking place, a group of Florida agents would be sealing off the bridge that connected the island to the mainland, trapping the Suárezes on the island with no escape route.

Baker went on, "Evaldo and Preston will be waiting at the main entrance of the hotel for the Suárez brothers and their crew, who will load the drugs. Of course, they will be armed, but Evaldo and Preston will not have weapons."

Did Baker know that the one time I had held a real gun was when the judge forced me to go duck hunting? When I tried to object, he laughed and said, "All lawyers should learn how to shoot, but since you do not know, you would be an added danger, not an asset."

All I could think of was the time when I was in sixth grade. My so called friends and classmates appointed me to watch at the door while they went out for a smoke. The teacher came back unexpectedly and we were nabbed. "Preston, I'm surprised that you are part of this scheme." My teacher, Mrs. Andrews said. 'You need to choose better friends. I am calling your mother."

"I've been working with the local law enforcement to put our plan together. There will be local police, state, and federal drug contingents, joining us. And, of course, Preston Ballard is here with his knowledge of Bolivia and his contacts with the Suárez drug operations."

He went on. "I want to emphasize that Evaldo and Preston are volunteer civilians, and not trained law enforcement officials. They will be unarmed and do not possess formal training. It is up to us to keep them out of harm's way."

I looked around and couldn't help but ask, "Is Evaldo coming to the meeting?"

Ed Baker paused, and, without answering my question went on as if he were filing an insurance claim. He made it clear that Evaldo and I would be ready to take the Suárez brothers to the sub-basement to show them the bags of cocaine wrapped in heavy plastic, and we would let them slit a bag open to taste it, just as I had seen in the movies. Then the Suárezes would call their men to begin loading the bags of cocaine on the elevator and move them to their panel trucks waiting outside. It would be Evaldo's job to take the cash payment from Arturo.

This event at my hotel would determine which of the two rival families—the Hausers or the Suárezes—would control the drug wealth. One of these families, my friends, the Hausers, was wealthy in land and cattle, and the Suárezes, my enemies, were wealthy from cocaine. It seemed clear, but it wasn't.

Was Evaldo trapped by his family's need to save its ranches, and, as a result, willing to play a dangerous game? Had he come to see that his family deserved a greater share of the profits from coca production?

Before today, the Hausers had only sold the refined coca paste to the Suárezes who then transported it to the huge U. S. markets, selling it for a much higher price than what they paid to the Hausers in Bolivia. The Hausers had kept their hands clean, or cleaner than the Suárezes at least.

How much longer could this unequal partnership between the two families go on? And how did I get caught in this war? And what about the plan I was part of—standing outside unarmed at The Blue Palm gate?

Ed Baker and the F.B.I. were going forward with the ghost ship plan—no ship, but real drugs—that would finally stop the Suárezes. I kept asking myself, was Evaldo using the F.B.I. to eliminate the Suárezes, so the Hausers could then have Bolivian coca production to themselves?

At Irobi, I had learned from the foreman that the Hausers had a bulldozer coming to speed up the construction of a new airfield. Did Arturo Suárez know about this new airfield, and did he understand it for what it was: a threat to the Suárez's total control of exporting cocaine to the U.S. markets?

Evaldo, surrounded by a large contingent of armed U.S. law enforcement agencies, would be exposed as using the drug raid to eliminate the Suárezes. This would allow the Hausers to move in and become the new major family controlling not only the Bolivian coca production but also the sales.

I was positive this war between two drug empires competing for control of the precious white powder was a deadly one. A scheme beyond reality which couldn't possibly work for Evaldo and his family unless Hernando and Arturo Suárez were killed during the F.B.I. raid.

After seeing Arturo give me the 'I know your name' look in San Ramón, I knew I would be a minor target tomorrow, but Evaldo would become the prime one.

The F.B.I. plan had too many loose ends. I was to stand outside the hotel with Evaldo, who so far had never been where the F.B.I. or anyone else had expected him to be. We, if Evaldo showed, might face crossfire from both sides once the Suárez crew started to load the drugs from the hotel into the waiting panel trucks. The F.B.I. and their respective law enforcement partners would be ready with the arrest warrants and guns, effectively ending the Suárez hegemony.

I didn't know who or what was to be trusted in this scheme. Without Delores, I didn't care if I lived or died.

I remembered putting off opening Delores's letter. One that might offer hope, but instead, left me in despair.

Delay or procrastination has often been my response when I am afraid. I had a similar feeling now. I had been almost hopeful before I knew the F.B.I.'s plan. One which depended on the appearance of a trusted, but false friend, Evaldo, and me, his Gringo idiot at the Blue Palm, the property that was now half mine and was nothing more than a payoff for my loss of Delores.

Ed Baker had still not answered my questions about Evaldo, who was absent when the meeting was coming to an end.

Queenie, Charley, and Ed had avoided looking at me most of the meeting. But by the end they met me with slaps on my back and encouraging phrases such as: "You'll be fine! Don't worry. We have your back. This is not a new rodeo for us.""

****

I went back to my trailer at Sunnyside and packed a bag with my toothbrush and a change of clothes, then drove back to the hotel.

Sandy Lefcourt had given me a large bunch of keys, with small white tags attached to identify each of them. I found the master key to the large double doors at the main entrance and went inside. Maybe I was going to spend the night, maybe my last night, in my hotel. Maybe my last night if I survived the raid.

The local police had made sure no hotel staff were allowed on the grounds or inside the hotel. The power for lights and air conditioning had been left on, anticipating the arrival the next day of the crew who would bring up the bags of cocaine from the sub-basement. The planning seemed fragile to me. It would never work.

I knew there was a small room tucked away in an alcove off the main lobby that was used for emergencies. It did not seem hurricane proof. It had a bed, with a small bath and white towels folded to look like some kind of bird. If, during the raid, there were a medical emergency, the room could be used, I thought, until a doctor or coroner arrived.

As I walked in, I could look across the lobby and see the hallway where the freight elevator was hidden out of sight. In my imagination, I was still in my bloody apron, standing in front of the open elevator door looking at Delores, who was studying some notes. She would look up and say those first words, ones that I would always remember, "Are you Preston Ballard?"

I wouldn't sleep if I survived the night. I knew that the bar was nearby.

I switched on some lights, bringing out the sparkle of the chandeliers, and walked to the end of the lobby. It led to a smaller area filled with tables and chairs in front of the bar, with its tall counter in front of the rows of bottles of all kinds; from whiskeys to imported wines.

I was surprised that the alcohol hadn't been carried away during the renovations.

I went behind the counter, found a glass and poured myself a stiff double shot of Jameson's Irish whiskey, the judge's favorite. I threw it back, then poured another before I went back out to the main lobby.

With the glass in my hand, I sat down at one of the tables, sipping my drink as I looked around. Everything I could see belonged to me—half of it, anyway— from the oriental carpets to the ivory inlay that edged the large counter where guests checked in belonged. Half of it was all mine. I couldn't help thinking that would surprise the judge, but then came the thought that he probably already knew about it. I was paranoid, but not about drug dealers and friends but also about the woman I loved. Everyone seemed to know more than I did.

Since it was my life on the line, I had to deal not only with what was going to happen in the morning, but also how deeply I was implicated in the case against the Suarez cartel. Did Arturo Suarez already know my secret identity as a mole working for the FBI? Did the FBI really have my back covered? Where was

Evaldo Hauser? How could we expect the Suarez clan to just peacefully show up in the morning to pick up millions of dollars worth of cocaine, as if they were picking up groceries?

23.

So, I was at my post on the circular driveway in front of the hotel. Ed Baker had told me to wait for the Suárez brothers who, Ed explained, would be driving up in rented SUVs. They would have bodyguards as well as men to bring up the bags of cocaine from the sub-basement of the hotel and load them into panel trucks. Arturo would have the cash payment for the cocaine, half a million in Ben Franklins, packed in a metal suitcase for Evaldo. With this transaction, the Suárezes would believe they were dealing with the major player in the Bolivian cocaine drug business.

The cameras hidden outside the hotel would record everything.

Ed Baker had told me in the meeting that I might be the one who would be handed the money from the Suárezes, since Evaldo had still not made an appearance.

I said that there was no way Arturo Suárez would hand over that much cash to me. Ed said not to worry; he was sure that Evaldo would soon show up. And besides, the drugs were stored in my hotel. This fact of my now owning the hotel, in and of itself, Ed had said, was proof that the Suárezes trusted me.

"Just think of yourself as the bagman," he had said.

Arturo Suárez would check out the drugs stored in the hotel and once he gave his approval, the drugs would be loaded into the Suárez panel trucks to be sold later for a fortune to American drug dealers.

The local law enforcement had been posted at a secluded area near what was called Limestone Pool. We waited for a phone call that would warn us that Arturo Suárez and his crew were on their way.

Evaldo had still not shown up. I don't know why I was surprised. It was good that I didn't care any longer, since I was sure that I had been targeted as someone to watch…or kill. Why go on living without Delores? Death would "kindly stop for me."

Emily Dickinson had the right words for my feeling that death would be a kind end after all I had been through.

While I waited for the call that the Suarezes were on their way, Ed had decided to wait with me before taking his post. He walked up to wait with me for the phone call warning us that the Suárezes were closer. I asked him, "When is Evaldo coming?"

"Don't worry, we're sure he's on his way. All you need to do is to wait for the Suárezes to come."

So, we waited, in silence. Did the F.B.I. know where Evaldo was or was I just being kept in the dark again.

Ed's cell hummed. He listened and then turned to me, "Ten minutes and they will be here. And stop worrying. Arturo Suárez knows who you are, the owner of the Blue Palm, and he trusts you or he wouldn't be using your hotel as the central repository for his drugs.. I'll be hidden at the back."

I watched him go, then stood there alone, wondering what my first words to Arturo and his crazy brother Hernando would be. I settled for "Don't shoot. It's me, Preston Ballard, Evaldo's friend. San Ramón, remember?"

After a few more tortuous minutes, I heard the motorcade of SUV's and panel trucks as the Suárez caravan swung into view. The lead SUV was moving slowly toward me with men, who, I was sure, held automatic weapons ready to fire. Behind the dark windows of one of the SUVs, I knew, were Arturo and Hernando Suarez.

The caravan came to a slow stop in front of me. One of the men in the lead SUV jumped out and ran over and tapped on the window of the last SUV.

The door opened and Hernando got out, looking around. He spotted me and whispered something to Arturo who then got out of another SUV. Hernando pointed at me. They both smiled and gave me a friendly wave before walking toward me.

Then I saw another figure. It was Evaldo. The Suarez brothers saw the shocked look on my face and started laughing.

"He didn't want to come," Hernando said. "He met an old girlfriend and wanted to stay for a visit, but we wouldn't let him."

The three of them came up and stopped. I took a deep breath.

"So, how was the trip?"

Arturo looked around and said, "Where are the drugs?"

"In the hotel. We can go in the front door."

Crazy Hernando asked, "Is it locked?"

I held up my ring of keys. As you know, I'm the owner."

Arturo turned and yelled at the men waiting in the other vehicles, "Miguel, keep a sharp lookout.."

A man waved, and several men posted themselves around Arturo's SUV.

The four of us started walking toward the large doors at the main entrance of the hotel. Evaldo was silent I could not guess what he felt Maybe he wanted to have someone else, me. answering the Suárezes questions about the layout of the hotel—where the drugs had been stored.

Inside, no one said anything as the two brothers looked around the vaulted Jazz Age lobby.

Arturo turned to me. "So, you own this place?"

"Half owner," I corrected.

"How old is it?"

"It was built in nineteen twenty-one by Lester Duncan, who made a fortune in soft drinks. He was known as the 'Cherry Smash King.' He went broke when the stock market crashed in twenty-nine. It was sold several times, and the last owner, Simon Khumar, bought it ten years ago.

Hernando laughed. "What happened to your girlfriend?"

"She's in Switzerland."

"Is she still Khumar's wife?

"Yes."

Arturo said "Stop the history lesson and love story.. We need to hurry."

Hernando gave me a disgusted look that clearly said, 'How can an undeserving shit like you have all the luck?'

I pointed down the lobby. "The elevator is this way."

The Suárez brothers, I was sure, had been keeping tabs on me and already knew all about Delores and her gift of the hotel. They also seemed to know before I told them that she was in Switzerland and not waiting for me. Their questions were poisoned probes, trying to trip me up.

The freight elevator was hidden in an alcove. The four of us got on. It rumbled down to the sub-basement.

Evaldo, standing beside me, said nothing, but what could he say with the killer brothers there?

The door opened. Directly in front of us were the bags of cocaine stacked in rows on a large sideboard.

Arturo nodded to Hernando, who pulled out a knife and walked over to the cocaine and slit open a bag at one end. The white powder spilled out. Hernando tasted it and then walked down the row of bags, slit open another bag and then looked back at Arturo.

"It's good, come and taste it for yourself."

Arturo stepped off the elevator and walked over to Hernando. They started whispering.

Evaldo waited with me in the elevator and grabbed my arm. In a rushed whisper he said, "Sorry I was late. They made me stay with them so I could not call you. The money is in Arturo's SUV in a large metal suitcase. Their men will bring the drugs out.

And only then will Arturo signal to give you the money. When all the drugs have been loaded, Arturo and Hernando will drive away. When that happens start running like hell for cover."

Evaldo broke off suddenly. Arturo and Hernando had turned and were looking at us.

Arturo yelled, "Hey, what's going on with you two? What are you talking about?"

Evaldo shrugged and gestured toward me. "He's worried."

"About what?"

"He thinks you're going to shoot him."

Hernando broke into a big smile. "We thought about it, but the coca is good, so we decided to do business instead."

The brothers walked toward us, arms extended. and after a few slaps on the back and with oaths of eternal brotherhood, we pledged to be friends for life. Hernando made a grim joke, "However short it might be."

We were soon outside.

Arturo gave the signal, and I followed the crew back down to the sub-basement.

They loaded the bags in large leather slings and began carrying them back up on the elevator.

When all the coca bags had been loaded into the waiting panel trucks, Arturo pressed a button and the back of his SUV popped open. He walked over and pulled out a large metal suitcase. He propped it up and opened the case.

Evaldo looked at it and said, "I'm sure it's all there," then Arturo nodded and even smiled.

I was impressed. I had never seen so much cash in my life. Evaldo snapped the suitcase shut.

Arturo handed Evaldo a small key for the suitcase, and said, "Until next time, my friend."

Arturo and Hernando got back in their SUV and the other vehicles started their engines. All drove toward the front gate in the direction of the island's bridge.

Evaldo lifted his hand, and then after thirty seconds of waving goodbye, he started running. I was right behind him.

Ed Baker emerged from his hiding place beyond the front steps of the hotel.

Pointing toward his cell phone, he meant that he had recorded it all.. I was sure that he had taken pictures of the crew loading the cocaine in the panel trucks and had caught the exchange of the money for the cocaine.

We stood on the veranda of the hotel, watching as the SUVs and panel trucks disappeared, heading toward the bridge.

What the Suárez brothers didn't know was that the state police had thrown up a barricade to block their escape from the island and were waiting to make a big bust of historic proportions: a cocaine seizure and the arrest of the Suarez brothers who headed the largest Mexican cartel.

But, as Ed Baker had once remarked, and I agreed, Arturo Suárez had not survived in the drug trade by being stupid. He had somehow learned—how we never knew—that there was a roadblock at the bridge. He also knew, somehow, about the private, almost invisible, dirt road that circled the island to a pier on the ocean side. No one suspected that the Suarez brothers knew about this dirt road. However, we learned, Arturo Suárez had not missed this fact. I was so preoccupied with my own anxieties about Delores and the whole nightmare operation that the dirt road never rose to the working part of my brain and I never mentioned it to Ed Baker.

As the line of vehicles approached the bridge to the mainland, Arturo's SUV stopped and waited. He must have heard the gunfire at the bridge so he ordered his driver to veer off onto the private dirt road, hidden in the tall grasses, leaving their people and the product in the panel trucks to be arrested. The Suarezes had to cut their losses. Their lives meant more than the cocaine they had just paid for.

When the shooting started at the bridge, Arturo turned onto the dirt road that led to the old pier on the ocean side of the island, where they had a speedboat waiting. He had a backup plan because he never trusted anyone or anything.

Back at the hotel, we listened to the gunfire, but remained unaware of that two of the Suárezes had escaped. The gunfire at the bridge died down and then ended.

After what seemed a long time but was not more than fifteen minutes, the abandoned drivers and guards came walking back from the bridge in handcuffs and sat on the lawn in a large circle in front of the hotel, waiting to be transported to a local jail.

I was amazed to see someone I knew in handcuffs. It was Gunny, the marine friend of President Martin at the Community College. It wasn't until later that I would understand the full meaning of why Gunny was sitting out on lawn, handcuffed and with his arm in a sling.

I stood on the veranda of the Blue Palm and listened as the sound of sirens on road that led to the bridge grew louder and louder. Based on the sound of gunfire back at the bridge, I guessed there must have been multiple injuries. Mostly on the side of the bad guys, I hoped, but I didn't see any.

I guessed that the F.B.I. had hustled off whoever of the Suarezes they caught to a secure location.

It wasn't until the next day that we knew what had happened. Evaldo and I were talking to Sandy Lefcourt, who immediately understood, and drove Evaldo, Ed Baker and me on the dirt road that circled around the island to the old pier that fronted the ocean, and long ago had fallen out of use. We saw the black SUV was parked by the pier where Arturo and

Hernando had abandoned it and boarded their waiting speed boat.

This was the road I had used almost every day on my five-mile run when I was a part time summer worker at the Blue Palm. Then it hit me again that this was a fact that I should have reported to Ed Baker—the escape route.

How could I have forgotten about that dirt road? And how did Arturo Suárez find out about it? Does the criminal mind work in entirely different ways or was I the most stupid, most naïve person on earth.

The Suárezes had not been able to take the bags of cocaine with them, so they'd lost a fortune in sales on the streets, and the F.B.I. had confiscated all the Suárezes' money in the metal suitcase.

Queenie and Charley spread the word on the streets of Savannah about the Ghost Ship scam, which made the local dealers furious and made the Suárez brothers look foolish for being duped. We would learn later they had somehow evaded capture in the States and made it back to one of their ranches in the Beni, where they were sending out word that the Hausers and their Gringo friend, me, would be paying with their lives.

24.

I was relieved to learn that I would not be called to testify in the trial of the men who were arrested during the drug raid at the Blue Palm. I knew from my law courses that the intricacies of probable cause and witness reliability had kept me from being called to the witness stand. The invisible hand of the judge was probably at work.

As it turned out, most of the men arrested had pled guilty in exchange for lower sentences.

But even avoiding the witness stand, I still felt that the entire Bolivian experience was, at least for me, a disaster. No matter how the F.B.I. and the law firm explained it, they had lied to me at almost every step of the way. Evaldo's first phone call, which asked me to help with his dying father, had been a lie. Amaya Wheeler's presentation of the assignment in Bolivia as a step up in the firm's ladder, to Ed Baker's asking me to write reports on the Bolivian cocaine trade would take a lifetime to come to terms with.

And of course, Delores's command not to come back had made me determined to come back, even if it had almost killed me. All lies at different levels. Some that I told myself.

I was tired of looking over my shoulder.

I started a regular routine running the dirt road that circled the island, but it wasn't clearing my head as it used to.

One day, as I was finishing my run, I decided to do and extra mile and keep running to the Cuba Libre Bar to talk things over with the owner. I thought Felix Guzman might have some information about Arturo Suárez. He always knew more than I did.

I thought Arturo would let things cool down before sending one of his hired guns to kill me. I was wrong. He did not wait.

Just in front of the Cuba Libre, as I was running up the drive, a car slowed down and shots were fired. But the shooter's aim was bad and the bullet only grazed my shoulder. I staggered and fell, which was good because a second shot followed, just missing my head. I was shocked but at the same time, I was not.

Felix Guzman had warned me this would happen before I went to Bolivia.

He had learned that Arturo and Hernando Suárez wanted me dead. And a part of me wanted to be dead too.

"Go far away, my friend," Guzman had advised. "Leave the island and the Blue Palm Hotel. Never stay too long in one place because Arturo Suárez will never forget."

Guzman was the head of the small Cuban community near my hometown, Clover, where I grew up. But he knew things beyond his beloved Cuba. His Cuba Libre was known as a clearinghouse for all sorts of news, a place where enemies could meet and be reconciled and secrets hidden and revealed.

Sometimes gunfire would break out in the parking lot, oaths would be shouted, and blood would be shed.

Through it all the Cuba Libre remained untouched, too valuable to all parts of the political and legal and criminal spectrum to be shut down.

Judge Talley had taken me there, after I gave in and reluctantly took his offer to pay for my law school where I would become close friends with Evaldo Hauser whose family-owned cattle ranches in Bolivia.

"You can go to the Cuba Libre and learn things you can't learn in law school, Preston," the judge had said. "Make friends with Guzman and do what he says. And always leave before the shooting starts."

Guzman had called me soon after the big drug bust, saying he had some useful information.

"We should talk, but be careful," Guzman had warned. "You need to know this. I have news regarding the drug raid at the Blue Palm. Arturo Suárez has put the word out. You are a marked man."

I was hoping his news might be about Delores. Why not know about her too.

Delores had left no forwarding address, except with Sandy and Ann Lefcourt.

"Forget Delores Khumar," Guzman had advised. "You need to concentrate on staying alive. Think about Alaska or the other side of the moon."

"I have to find her first."

"You can't find anybody when you're dead. Which reminds me, your tab is over the limit."

"I'm broke."

"How can that be possible? I heard you're a rich man."

How did Guzman know that? How did everyone always know more than I did?

"I'll see you here tomorrow," I said.

"I hope so. You'll be lucky to live through the night."

But I did make it through the night and had spent a week at the hotel, trying to think straight and running every day across the one bridge that connected the island to the mainland. On one run, I had almost reached Guzman at the Cuba Libre.

I had wanted to get my thoughts lined up before I met with him but couldn't because I was shot. Guzman was looking out his office window and saw me stumbling in my bloody shirt, my useless arm swinging beside me. He signaled for me to come in and I staggered in.

Somehow, I made through the beaded curtain into the large room, where I could see dim figures moving in the thick smoke of Cuban cigars. A long mirror behind the bar reflected the room.

On the other side of the room, behind a large potted palm, was the door to Guzman's office. He was staring at me with his slow, sad eyes.

"Have a drink.. It may be your last one."

"No thanks." I could feel my legs starting to buckle. "I want to talk to you but I am about to pass out."

Without answering Guzman reached behind the potted palm and touched something. There was a hiss, and the door to his office slid open.

Bracing myself against tables and chairs, I moved toward a sofa in the middle of the room. Filing cabinets stood against the wall with the drawers left half open. Stacks of papers and folders were on a couple of large tables, along with cups of coffee half full, cigar butts, stale donuts on paper plates, and old newspapers. The overall impression was of a place where everything was constantly changing but always remaining the same—exactly the way I felt, ruined but the same.

Guzman helped me take off my bloody shirt and began examining the wound in my shoulder with tentative touches.

"You're lucky," he said. "The bullet missed the bone and went all the way through. The next time you won't be so lucky. "You have no idea what you have done.

You helped in the raid that almost sent the Suárez brothers to prison, especially that crazy brother."

"I was just one of a team. Just one of the backup teams. Just one."

"Well, it was a dangerous job—that ghost ship scheme. The plan was bound to go wrong. You met Suárez brothers in Bolivia and now they know you betrayed them."

Guzman reached under the sofa I was sitting on and pulled out a bottle of rum.

"You're going to need this."

I took several long pulls of rum as Guzman began moving around the room looking for something he couldn't seem to find. After a moment he gave his forehead a smack.

"Stupid! The needle is in the refrigerator." He went over to a small fridge hidden in the corner of the room and pulled out a first aid kit.

"Bullet wounds always feel better with Novocain, don't you think?" He filled a syringe and stuck me.

"I wouldn't know."

"This was a warning from Arturo Suárez. The next time he won't miss. Go far away, my friend, and start over. I had to leave my Cuba, my country and my woman.

You must do the same."

"I can't leave."

"Won't she go with you?"

"No. She can't leave her husband. He's dying."

"You should have known all that."

"She told me I could never understand her decision to stay with him."

Guzman shrugged.

"Good. Well, that means she's loyal. Sometimes a man must accept what happens, even when he doesn't like it. But that hotel is a very dangerous place. And, as I understand it, the Khumars left some time ago. They must have known something was coming."

"I'm not sure what they knew."

I remembered Guzman had lost friends in the failed Bay of Pigs, so he knew about grief.

To get him away from the subject of Delores Khumar and me, I pointed to some photographs on the wall. "Who are those people?"

"Soldiers, from the Bay of Pigs. Most are dead now."

"Have you accepted that?"

"I accept what I have to accept."

"I am trying to do that as well."

"Then there is nothing more I can do."

Guzman put the first aid kit on one of the tables, and then turned back, again looking at me for a moment with those slow, sad eyes.

"You can spend the night on the sofa. I will call a doctor who can be here in the morning to sew you up and give you some antibiotics. Then you will have to leave. Drink some more rum and go to sleep."

He pointed to a pillow and blanket at the end of the sofa.

"Get some rest. You'll need it."

The door opened and I could see Guzman's assistant waiting as he nervously looked around.

Guzman stepped out and I heard him say "He won't believe that the Suárezes have a target on his back."

The assistant asked, "What did they say?"

"What we all knew they would say: Preston Ballard is an idiot. He tried to send the Suárezes to prison."

The Novocain and the rum were putting me under, but I did hear the assistant ask Guzman again if I really doubted that I was a marked man.

Guzman shrugged. "If the bullet didn't convince him, what would? Nothing must happen to him here." Guzman continued. "Besides, he wants to find his inamorata, no matter what."

"You mean…?"

"Khumar's wife, Delores."

"Well, it's his own funeral."

"Whatever the Suárezes are planning, it has started. If Ballard stays here any longer, he's a dead man. "I told him to leave the country, anywhere on earth but Bolivia.

He's brought this down on himself. The indictment of the Suárezes, if it ever happens, might calm things down. We want to keep bringing our Cuban friends here. We learned a long time ago that there is always trouble in this business of dealing with refugees."

"So," the assistant asked, "the drug shipment came in, Evaldo Hauser paid for the drugs, the hidden cameras caught it all and the trap closed, bang, like that?"

I heard Guzman clap his hands.

"I understand it all went down at the Blue Palm. The Suárezes feared that Ballard, the same Gringo whom they had met in Bolivia and who had seen their drugs packed in the carcasses of the cattle, knew too much. They must have thought that it was Ballard's idea that an old hotel on a small island off the Florida coast would be safer than Savannah or Miami. The old hotel would not be under surveillance. It seemed the perfect place. The Suárezes thought they had the deal all arranged and were persuaded to buy the drugs stored at the Blue Palm from the Hausers. I am sure the drugs and the cash were supplied by the F.B.I. Everybody thought it was a perfect plan."

The room began to spin around from the rum and Novocain, and their voices faded. I didn't wake up for a long time.

*****

The next day I was back in my trailer. The doctor had said the infection from the wound was spreading and dangerous. Part of me wanted the infection to go untreated, but there was too much to settle about the hotel, and I needed to settle things with Sandy and Ann Lefcourt first.

Guzman had recommended a doctor who would ask no questions.

By the next week my infection had turned my shoulder purple with red streaks running down my arm. I began going every day to a small clinic for multiple shots of antibiotics.

One late afternoon, in the doctor's waiting room, I was the last patient left on the doctor's list of patients to be seen. No one was around except one nurse who was busy filling out forms.

A janitor came in to empty the trash and mop the floors. He moved toward me, his head down, intent on his work. He wrung out his mop and looked up, then he saw me. It was, to my surprise, Junior Jackson, who years ago had shot the Blue Jays with me at Uncle Virgil's farm.

"Hey, Junior," I said. "Recognize me?"

Junior turned his head sideways and squinted. Then came up close. "Well, I'll be damned! It's… Preston…?"

"Right. Preston Ballard."

Junior stepped closer. "I thought so… We shot those birds for your Uncle. I heard what your mother made you do. Who would do such a thing?" Junior put his mop down.

"What brings you here?

I pointed to my shoulder and said, "Somebody shot me."

Junior took a step back and gave me a closer look. "How are you feeling"?

"I'm doing better. I heard you were doing time?"

"I am. But judge Talley got me a reduced sentence after another man confessed to pulling the trigger. Now I'm on 'good behavior' and work release."

I laughed, and said, "That's like my doctor. He doesn't call it work release, but in another week and he says he'll release me."

Junior looked me over and said, "I hope so. To be honest, you don't look so good."

A week later, I had my last visit with the doctor.

"How's the pain?"

"I am feeling better," I said.

The doctor gave an indifferent shrug and sent me home.

"Call me if there is any change. And finish those antibiotics."

That one night before the drug raid at the Blue Palm had been enough. I didn't want to spend another at the hotel, so I continued living in my trailer.

The day after my last appointment with the doctor, my phone hummed. It was Sandy Lefcourt.

"Ann and I want you to come for dinner. How about tomorrow night? We have a lot to talk about, don't you think? The three of us own an old hotel now. How about it?

Our suite in the hotel is being remodeled, so come to the Far Cottage."

I didn't want to say that the Far Cottage was the last place on earth I wanted to meet anybody... but, thinking that it would simplify things, I went.

We sat outside the Far Cottage. Ann and I talked while Sandy grilled steaks.

I tried to ignore my memories of Delores. They went floating up over the grill.

Sandy had a large pitcher of margaritas on the table. We were relaxed and soon I fell under the influence of Sandy and Ann's hospitality. I asked about the on-going restoration of the hotel.

"It's almost completed," Sandy explained. "We were anxious about the damage the drug business might cause to the hotel. Not only to the building, but to its future as a

destination for the kind of guests we need."

This mention of financial vulnerability gave me an opening to ask what arrangements Delores had made about their situation at the hotel.

Before Sandy could answer, I said "I appreciate what you and Ann are doing. If you can go on the way we are, with the two of you running things, we can draw up a contract. With the two of you as co-owners and running the hotel and me as sort of a silent partner. I want to do other things."

I paused, not sure how to go on.

Ann looked at Sandy and then said, "What about the hotel? You could have a

suite of rooms here as a backup?"

I shook my head.

"No, I need a place that's different. Maybe in another country I could never blend in. live far away, but I'm not sure what I'll do or where I will live.

"Just take care of the paperwork and I'll sign it. Of course, you may have other plans. Just let me know. Take your time to decide. You don't have to answer now. But I am out of here."

Ann gave me a concerned look.

"Preston, are you sure about this? I mean…" She stopped, as if I would know what she meant.

"What are you worried about?"

Ann took a deep breath. "I mean, what about Delores? Is this what she wanted?"

"I wrote to Delores after I read her letter about her gift of the hotel. She made it clear she wasn't coming back."

No one said anything, and then I realized I had echoed Delores's own words to me— "Don't come back".

There was silence. I felt a surge of conviction inside me telling me that I was doing the right thing.

"This is what I want, not just what Delores wanted."

Sandy and Ann looked at each other. Ann reached out and took his hand and nodded.

"Yes, this is what we both want," Sandy said. "And thank you. Not many people are given a grand old hotel, or even half of one."

"You don't have to tell me."

I started to get up and say goodnight, but Ann said, "There is one more thing.

Have you been inside the hotel?"

"Just the night before the raid. I really couldn't see much."

"Simon wanted a complete restoration of the hotel. He left enough money to finish it. The first half, which was the inside, has just been completed: new furniture, plumbing, lighting, painting. All new, but in keeping it reminiscent of its 1910s original design. Delores and I had agreed on what needed to be done long before she left. We can do the second half, the landscaping and gardens as well new tennis courts and swimming pools, next year. When we finish, you should come back from wherever you have landed and take a look."

Sandy added, "We do hope you come back."

Ann smiled and I could tell there was more, so I asked, "Anything else?"

"To celebrate, we've planned a big party for the New Year with many of Simon's old friends from Europe, New York, Palm Beach, and San Francisco, plus Sao Paulo, Buenos Aires, and even the Hausers from the Beni. Maybe two hundred or so guests.

We included the address of Delores's new orphanage and hospital for people who want to donate."

Sandy added, "We're sorry to spring this on you, but the invitations have been sent out, giving people six months to make travel arrangements. You are now an owner with us of the hotel, and we need you to be here."

"I don't know where I will be in six months. Just let me know."

We stood up.

Ann gave me a careful look and said, "Promise me you will take care of that shoulder. Sepsis can be serious."

I left Sandy and Ann feeling more confused but reassured by their warmth and kindness.

Back at the mobile home park, I poured two shots of Makers Mark in a paper cup and tried to ignore the pain in my shoulder that was throbbing. I went outside and sat down in my front yard.

My phone buzzed. It was my mother.

"Preston, I've been trying to call. I wanted to call you and say we're leaving for New Zealand next week, so I may not see you for a while. The judge has real estate investments there."

"I didn't know the judge had any interest in New Zealand."

"There are many things you don't know about the judge." She cut off the connection.

I heard the waves hitting the shore. A half line of a sonnet ran through my head:

"So do our minutes hasten to their end."

I had no idea what my end would be. None in the world.

My life went on, disconnected in a thousand ways that should have been predictable but were not.

The big party that Sandy and Ann were planning had to be cancelled as the Covid virus spread. The Bolivian cocaine trade became more and more chaotic. Evaldo wrote to Sandy and Ann, but not until sometime later to me.

The small growers in the Beni were dying. One day a grower would be ready to harvest his crop, and the next the virus would strike, and entire families would be wiped out. Buyers in the States paid exorbitant prices as production plummeted.

I was out of the loop and was relieved.

Florida remained the home of the Big Crazies. Masks and no masks, college kids on the beaches. Many retirees were wiped out. It was like Poe's "Masque of the Red Death," people were having fun one moment and dead the next.

My mother and judge Talley stayed in New Zealand for a year, and then flew back to Florida just before the vaccine shots became available. They were both infected, either during the flight or when they landed, and were immediately quarantined. They died within a week of each other.

I inherited my mother's house and put it on the market.

My father's brother, Uncle Virgil, came to the judge's funeral and then stayed for my mother's a week later. We had a couple of long sessions late at night. I told him I thought his letter during the war, when he took over the ammunition train which miraculously did not blow up, had inspired me. I know I could not have jumped in an abandoned, runaway ammunition train and brought it to a safe stop.

He laughed and said, "It was insane. I never told anybody that two days after I got back to my company, another train of ours blew up outside a small French village and wiped out half the town. I had never before or after done anything as impulsive as that."

We talked for another fifteen minutes, and then Uncle Virgil stood up and said goodbye.

I hesitated, and then said "One more question. Are you still shooting Blue Jays out of your pecan trees?"

His eyes lit up, and he smiled.

"Once in a while. Why don't you come for a visit, and we can shoot them together? I was shocked that day by your mother more than I knew how to say. I'd seen boys beaten with leather belts, me included, but no Blue Jays roasted and served to a child, a son."

When Uncle Virgil left, it was as if all the connections to my earlier life had been severed. I could feel myself floundering, starting to go in one direction and then changing my mind and going in another. The only connection to my earlier life, the life of childhood and high school, my mother, and judge Talley, was Ann Glazer Lefcourt.

I called Ann and suggested grilling more steaks at the Far Cottage, and this time I would bring the steaks. She said she would make a salad and Sandy would take care of the drinks. She suggested New York strips, and a good red wine from the Elk Hill Vineyard in Virginia.

"Will it be okay if I invite someone else?" Ann asked. "She lives out west, somewhere in Montana. We were in nursing school together, but she has never visited me here in Florida.

"Her name is Gwen. She lost her husband in a freak accident. He was on his new motorcycle and probably going too fast when a deer jumped out from the woods. He lost control and hit a tree. Gwen was left with two little boys, Jess and Mac, who are, as she puts it, the local troublemakers."

Ann was careful to say, "Don't worry. I'm not fixing either one of you up. You're both wrecks, I'm sorry to say."

We were wrecks, at least I was. Ann introduced me as an out of work lawyer and absentee hotel owner. I'm sure Ann thought Gwen was someone I would enjoy hanging out with.

Gwen had pale brown hair, blue eyes, and wore faded jeans and a gray sweater with a string of pearls. She seemed to be always looking out toward the western horizon.

She had left her two young sons with her mother back home in Montana. She was more worried about her mother than the boys, who could ride their ponies and keep up with the big horses.

Gwen was preoccupied with how they were doing. Their family had moved out west from New England during the Depression in the thirties, and she had been visiting relatives outside of Boston before coming to Florida to see Ann and meet Sandy.

As I started to leave, Gwen wrote down her address and cell phone number and said that if I wanted to see the West I could come out and spend some time at her family's ranch.

"Does that mean I'd have to ride a horse?"

"Only if you want to. Ann said you were a regular cowboy in Bolivia."

"I think Ann is seriously confused."

"Why don't you come anyway and find out for yourself?"

"You're sure. No expectations?"

"No expectations." I could see her trying not to smile.

I took a deep breath and said, "Thanks, I might do that."

The End

ABOUT THE AUTHOR

Roy Robbins is an award-winning playwright with four plays and, more recently, a book of poems to his credit. North is his debut novel. Robbins studied poetry with James Dickey at the University of South Carolina, theater in New York, and literature at the University of Virginia. His most recent work, a book of poetry entitled Poster Art Nights, was published in 2015. Robbins lives in rural Virginia with his wife, the author Susan Pepper Robbins, who writes novels about the South and teaches writing at Hampden-Sydney College.

ABOUT THE PRESS

Unsolicited Press is based out of Portland, Oregon and focuses on the works of the unsung and underrepresented. As a womxn-owned, all-volunteer small publisher that doesn't worry about profits as much as championing exceptional literature, we have the privilege of partnering with authors skirting the fringes of the lit world. We've worked with emerging and award-winning authors such as Shann Ray, Amy Shimshon-Santo, Brook Bhagat, Kris Amos, and John W. Bateman.

Learn more at unsolicitedpress.com. Find us on twitter and instagram.

www.ingramcontent.com/pod-product-compliance
Lightning Source LLC
LaVergne TN
LVHW091818110525
810975LV00035B/467